SISSY HUSBAND

4

A cuckold sissy and his strict dominant wife

by

Lady Alexa

Lady Alexa Publications

Also by Lady Alexa

A Sissy Cuckold Husband
Sissy Husband 3

Becoming Joanne
Becoming Joanne 1
Becoming Joanne 2
Becoming Joanne 3

Femboy Love
Femboy Love 1

Feminized and Pretty
Feminized and Pretty 1
Feminized and Pretty 3
Feminized and Pretty 4

Forced Feminization

Forced Feminization Bundle 1

Lockdown Feminization
Lockdown Feminization 3
Lockdown Feminization 1

Sissy femboy transgender husband
SIssy Husband 1
Sissy Husband 4

Sissy Princess
Sissy Princess 2
Sissy Princess 1

Stepmother's Sissy
Stepmother's Sissy
Stepmother's Sissy 2
Stepmother's Sissy 3

Standalone
A Very Dominant Woman
Sissy Pink

Subscribe to my blog charting my real-life FLR and forced feminisation lifestyle with my feminised husband Alice here: www.ladyalexauk.com[1]
You can also subscribe to my newsletter from my blog by clicking on the side bar and entering your email: www.ladyalexauk.com

---

CONTENTS

Sissy Husband 4 is the fourth and final book of an updated re-telling of an earlier series called A Sissy Cuckold Husband which is now no longer available.

I revisit my older books from time to time to update the covers and some of the inner text. While updating my A Sissy Cuckold Husband series, I noticed there was an alternative storyline within the plot – that of husband who visits professional mistresses to live out his sissy fantasy but keeps his femboy dreams a secret from his wife Gemma.

Once Gemma finds out her husband's desires to be a femboy sissy through his former girlfriend, Gemma and her new friend set about realising his and their dream. Her husband Paul pushes back as he tackles his inner societal programming that being a sissy femboy is somehow shameful despite his internal feelings.

The series now has more of a transgender awakening theme and of a mutually agreed relationship that satisfies everyone but is very different to what society considers the norm.

IN THIS FINAL BOOK *of the Sissy Husband series, we find Pansy formally Paul, now a full-time sissy for his wife Gemma. Gemma has made friends with Fiona, the Principal of an Institute for the Improvement of Sissies. Fiona not only enrols Pansy at her Sissy Institute, but helps Gemma on a more personal level to increase Pansy's sissification. And a big part of Pansy's sissification is Gemma finding a boyfriend to cuckold her husband Pansy with.*

Chapter 1: Surprise

Gemma squeezed the door handle down and pushed into Pansy's small bedroom trying to be quiet. Dr Fiona followed her in. They tiptoed to the small bed where Gemma's husband Pansy was curled up under pink sheets. He looked cute. His head was sunk deep into the printed image on the pillow of a cartoon princess.

Pansy's breathing came from the back of his throat, his mouth open. Gemma put her lips to his ear.

"Wake up, Pansy, we want to play."

His eyes flicked open, dazed and uncomprehending, not properly awake. She shook his shoulder and he sat up with a jump. His head turned one way and the other. "What? What?" He rubbed at the corner of an eye.

Gemma threw back the covers. His short pink baby-doll nightie was ruffled around his hips, his little caged penis displayed. It was small, soft and sleepy inside the pink resin prison. Dr Fiona flicked on the light. He closed his eyes tight and put his head into his hands.

Gemma took his hand. "Out you get, Pansy Princess, we want to play." Mischief danced in her voice.

He took his hands away from his eyes and looked at Gemma with red bleary eyes of incomprehension. He pulled the nightie over his penis cage and held it down.

Gemma pulled him around so he sat on the edge of the bed. He yawned, stretched his arms in the air, spotted Dr Fiona and froze with his arms up.

"Dr Fiona?" He lowered his arms and rubbed his eyes again as if not believing what he saw. He decided it was real. "What are you doing here?"

Dr Fiona put her hands on her hips, her face flicked with a flash of irritation. "That's an irrelevant and, I might say, an impertinent question for an insolent little girl to ask."

Pansy struggled to take in her words or the situation.

Gemma opened his small wardrobe. She shuffled through the dresses and skirts hanging on a thin metal bar until she found what she was looking for. She pulled it out and held it up for Dr Fiona to see, a wide satisfied grin on her face. She held a small cherry red dress. It had wide box pleats, one pleat was red the alternate white. The chest had a large white P on it. Two cherry-red pom-poms hung from the top.

"We're going to dress you up in this pretty cheerleader outfit, Pansy Princess." Gemma held it to his face. "You can do a little cheerleader song and dance for us when you're all dressed and pretty. And wave the pompoms, like an adorable little cheerleader girl."

Dr Fiona felt the dress, rubbing it between two fingers. "Exquisite, Gemma Sweetheart." She turned to Pansy and thought for a moment. "How about singing this for us? *I am a girly cheerleader, a pansy I've become, I want to suck off sissy girls and swallow all their cum.*"

Gemma kissed Dr Fiona full on the lips and lingered for seconds. "That was so good, Fiona. Did you just make it up?" Pansy's eyes widened in shock at seeing his wife and Fiona kiss passionately.

"Yes, Sweetheart. How about another chant for Pansy?" She thought again. "*I have a tiny clitty and I'm a pretty lass. I fondle sissy clits and I take them in my ass.*"

"Fiona, you're so funny." Gemma turned to Pansy. "Stand up, Princess, it's time to become an adorable cute little cheerleader."

He stood with a tired sullen reluctance, his shoulders slumped. He wasn't yet fully awake despite the disruption around him.

"She's such an adorable little girl in that baby-doll." Dr Fiona put two fingers under his penis cage. "And look how small this little thing is. A soft two-inch little clitty just like a real girl." She rubbed her fingers against his little balls. "And what have we here?" She looked in closer. "They are like two little acorns, Gemma sweetheart. You did the right thing bringing her to me. She is the perfect candidate for sissy school, short and girly with a tiny clitty and minuscule girly balls." Dr Fiona dropped his genitals with a shake of her head. "The sooner we fatten her up a little we put her into pretty little sissy dresses, the better. She's such a femboy."

"Speaking of which." Gemma handed her the hanger with the cheerleader dress on and then pulled Pansy's arms up. She unlocked and removed the chastity cage and put her hands on the hem of his light pink see-through nightie. She pulled it up to his chest. She drew it over his head and tossed it on the bed.

His stirring penis caught Dr Fiona's eye. "What do we have here?" She took the end between two fingers and rolled it. "How cute; she has a little erection starting. At least something is waking up."

Gemma and Dr Fiona gave dismissive laughs. Gemma returned to the wardrobe. She found a pair of panties in matching cherry-red. Gemma knelt, facing Pansy's erection. She planted a slow kiss on the end of his erection and giggled. She hooked the panties over his ankles. She drew them up his legs to his little penis and balls. She pulled them up tight, his erection poking the front out. He remained pliant and resigned although Gemma saw a glint of excitement in his eyes.

Gemma edged her hand inside his panties in one smooth movement. She smiled at him as she manipulated his erection down and then pulled his panties tight to smooth out the front. A small little bump was all that showed.

"We can't have an adorable little cheerleader girl with a tiny bulge in the front of her pretty panties." Gemma's face creased in an amused and tender way. She tapped the front of his panties in satisfaction and grinned up at him.

She picked up the cheerleader dress and pulled it over his head. He grumbled under his breath but didn't fight the inevitable. Tiredness and the inevitability defeated him. She tugged the top down to smooth it out. She traced the outline of the large white **P** on the chest with a red fingernail.

"P is for Pansy," she explained.

"P for Princess too," Dr Fiona added. "And Prissy, Pee-wee, Pickle, Pretty and Petal." She raised her eyebrows and moved into his face. "You're a pretty, prissy, pansy princess." She tickled him under his chin. "And don't you look like an adorable little cheerleader girl. Maybe we can find you a pretty sissy girl to play with. Tell me you want a cute sissy's clitty in your sissy vagina, Pansy."

Pansy blushed and looked to the floor. He stood still with his hands by his side as the two ladies waited for him to repeat what Dr Fiona asked.

"I want a sissy clitty in my ass." His voice was low and almost a mumble.

"Good, sissy girl." Gemma beamed and kissed him. She tweaked his face and then hugged him tight.

His cherry red top was like a vest and the dress pleats were wide. Three parallel red and white stripes ran around the bottom of the dress. Gemma slipped a pair of ankle-length white socks on his feet and light-coloured pink girl's training shoes.

Dr Fiona pulled on the side of his hair, her hands ran through his hair. She tugged it into a single side ponytail coming from one temple. She slid a pink elasticated band down her fingers and secured his ponytail with a twist. She did the same for the other side. The ponytails touched the tops of his shoulders on either side. Using the tips of her fingernails as a wide comb, she scratched the front of his hair down to his eyelashes. He blinked as his fringe flicked into his eyes.

Gemma took a tube of lipstick and twisted the tube. A bright pink stick emerged. With concentration etched on her face, she held it like an artist holding a paintbrush and glided it over his lips. She told him to push his lips together and mimed the movement for him, finishing with a bright smile. He pushed his lips together, smoothing out the lipstick.

"Hold your hands out flat, Pansy, Nails facing up," Dr Fiona said.

He held them out. She shook a small pink bottle and unscrewed the top. She took out the small brush attached to the lid and steadied one of his hands with her soft dark fingers. She ran the brush over his thumbnail with one smooth stroke down the middle. It was bright luminous pink. She filled in the sides and moved on to his next finger. She finished his nails off in the pink varnish.

Gemma unhooked the two pom-poms from the hanger and held them out for him to take. He took one in each hand.

"You'll carry these, Pansy Princess," Gemma said. "We're going downstairs now and you will do a cheerleader song and dance for us."

His shoulders drooped. "Do I have to? It's late."

She stroked his head and ran a hand over one ponytail. "Ah, poor Pansy, all sleepy-weepy." Gemma's face softened. "You're such an adorable pansy-puff; I'm going to keep you this way always. I don't want you in male clothes ever again."

His body stiffened. "That's not possible, I have to go into work."

Gemma tweaked his cheek. "Everything's possible, sissy femboy."

Dr Fiona took him by the wrist and led him downstairs, her eyes kindly and gentle. Gemma walked behind, watching with tender endearment as Pansy descended the stairs. She loved the way his little dress flicked up and then down like a parachute around his bare legs. Most of all, she loved his vulnerability and her absolute control.

Gemma pushed by Dr Fiona and Pansy in the downstairs hall and opened the living room door. Uplighters threw out a low light in contrast to the cold white brightness of the hall. Gemma's long tall shadow fell into the living room, dark against the surrounding dull yellow ambience.

Gemma went in, a conspirational grin pasted on her face. She stood back as Dr Fiona came in first, her hand around Pansy's wrist, the pom-poms flicking in his hand. They walked to the centre of the room, Pansy's head was down as he contemplated the upcoming humiliation.

"Look up, Pansy, be proud to be a sissy femboy," Dr Fiona said.

Pansy looked up, his eyes flat. They opened wide and he fell back, as if fainting. His assistant Jerome was sitting on the sofa. Jerome's rigid hands gripped the seat, mouth open wide, his eyes fixed on his boss. Jerome looked at Gemma in astonishment and back at his boss, dressed as a cheerleader. Jerome pressed his fingertips to his temples and appeared to have stopped breathing.

"Now you see my problem, Jerome, and why I needed a real man like you?" said Gemma. "My husband, your boss, is a sissy femboy pansy"

Chapter 2: Sissy Cheerleader

Jerome closed his mouth and looked and Gemma and then to Dr Fiona. He shivered once, a deep shudder that ran down his body to his feet. He got up, Dr Fiona placed a hand on his shoulder and pushed him back down. She raised a single finger to his face. "You can stay there, Jerome, you have nothing to worry about. Gemma's in charge here, not Pansy Paul."

"She's no longer Paul Paige but Pansy Princess," Gemma continued. "Say hello to Pansy Princess, Jerome."

Pansy's body closed up. His chest tightened, his knees touched together and his feet turned in.

Jerome's throat caught, struggling to take in what he was experiencing. His boss was dressed as a teenage girl. Jerome swallowed and composed himself. "Hello, Pansy Princess." He swallowed again. His eyes swivelled to Gemma before they settled on his boss then flowed up and down taking in the little dress, his boss's submissive body language and his hairstyle. There was too much to take in. The room was in silence. Jerome swallowed again, his mouth was clearly dry.

Dr Fiona clapped. "Well done, Jerome." Her eyes sparkled in the dull light. "Did you know that Pansy Princess has a tiny clitty and girly balls?"

Jerome's mouth fell open again.

"Would you like to see?" Dr Fiona said.

Jerome shook his head, his eyes fixed on his boss. He shook his head as he spoke. "I don't think that is a good idea."

"Of course it is, Jerome darling," said Gemma. I don't want you to feel guilty when we have sex. I want you to know how much I've suffered having to put up with my sissy husband's pathetic little clitty."

Gemma lifted the front of Pansy's dress who looked away to the door, his face screwed in anguish. Gemma pulled down the front of his panties and lifted his dress before looking back at Jerome with a wide grin. Pansy Paul's little erection poked forward, hard and small. "See," said Gemma. "Tiny."

Jerome looked away, then back. He didn't want to see it but couldn't help himself.

"Not like your magnificent masculine rod, is it, Jerome? Do you see what I have to put up with? A sissy girly husband with the tiniest little clitty and girly balls."

Pansy Paul's face went a dark red of humiliation and anger. Jerome stared ahead, unbelieving at what was going on.

Gemma pulled Pansy's panties to his ankles and shuffled him to stand closer to Jerome. Jerome froze at the proximity to his boss's tiny erection. Gemma held Pansy's skirt to his stomach and put her hand around his little balls. "She has the tiniest little erection, don't you think? Can you imagine what it's like for me to try to give her a blow job? It's like sucking on a straw. Not at all like yours, lover, I much preferred sucking on your massive cock. That's a real man's cock."

Pansy shot Gemma a look. "tell me you didn't?" he looked full at Jerome. "He's my assistant. You can't. You mustn't."

Gemma kissed his cheek. "Of course I did, pansy-puff. I sucked him off in the back room of the bar." Gemma's tone was like a mother talking to her little daughter. "Big Jerome's cock was so big, I couldn't get in all my mouth. I had to take it down my throat too."

Pansy's face fell. You blew my assistant? Are you mad?"

"No, just bored with what you had, Pansy. My stomach is so full of big Jerome's cum, I won't need to eat anything for a week. There was so much of it, I didn't think he was ever going to stop. He enjoyed having his boss's wife sucking him off."

Pansy's eyes narrowed and shot to Jerome who went scarlet. Gemma and Fiona giggled.

"My cute Pansy Princess," said Gemma. "You're so adorable, such a girly sissy." Gemma's voice was sweet and she then slapped Pansy across his face. Gemma put her hands on Pansy's shoulders and turned him to one side. He shuffled with the panties around his ankles. She aimed another swing across his other cheek and Pansy's head flew to one side with the blow. She kissed his cheek, soothing the redness from her slap. "My darling little sissy femboy."

Dr Fiona grabbed his ear and twisted hard and down. She bent him over, his dress lifted over his bare bottom. She slapped him hard across his buttocks while keeping him held down by a twisted ear. She twisted it further and Pansy squealed, *"Eeeeeeee."* Dr Fiona turned his ear 360 degrees. He squealed again, *"Waaaaaaaaah."*

Dr Fiona lifted her free arm and swung at Pansy's bare bottom with the force of her entire body. He screamed out. She rained spank after spank, his cheeks turning red. He yelped and squealed.

She pulled him up by one of his ponytails and bent his head back. Gemma looked into his eyes, close. She stroked the back of his head, her long fingers light on his head. "You look so pretty, girly sissy. Look at you, all decked out in a cute cheerleader dress. "My darling adorable little princess. I want to squeeze you up with love." Gemma hugged him.

Dr Fiona took Pansy's two side ponytails and pulled him further back so he was bent backwards. His little pleated dress lifted above his erection. Jerome watched the scenes unfolding from inches away, his face set fixed in a stunned expression.

Gemma bent down and looked in close to Pansy's erection. "My pansy sissy is excited by our attention." She tapped the end twice. "Don't tell me you don't enjoy being our pretty princess." She kissed the end of his erection with gentle affection. She grabbed his little balls. She dug her nails in, they sank into the soft skin of his groin. Pansy shrieked and Jerome jumped at the sound. Gemma maintained the squeeze, her eyes smiling sweetly. Gemma kissed the end of his nose and let go.

Pansy squealed, "Owww."

She touched his balls with a soothing rub and a concerned look. "Oh my poor darling Pansy, did that sting?" Her voice was full of compassion. She kissed his balls again, her mouth pushed between his balls and upper thigh. Her blond hair flicked then hung over his erection and the soft skin of his groin. "Let me kiss them better." She slurped two kisses. "There, there, is that all better now, sweet sissy boy?"

Jerome's eyes took in the spectacle. Pansy let out a breath, calming down, his sobs were gentle and tears glistened in his eyes but his face softened at his wife's loving attention.

Dr Fiona pulled him further back by his ponytails. Gemma took hold of his little erection and pulled it towards her. "I'm going to see how far I can stretch this little Miss Clitty, to make it longer. Three inches up to five? Maybe I can get it to six?" Gemma said.

"Go for six, sweetheart," Fiona said.

Gemma pressed a hand against the top of Pansy's thigh, her elegant hand splayed against his skin. Her red long fingernails made five little indents. She wrapped a thumb and finger around the little head of his erection and stretched his erection towards her. She pushed a counter pressure the other way against his thigh.

Pansy wailed in complaint, *"Eeeeeeeeeeeeeeeh."* Gemma pulled harder. She maintained the pressure, further and further, his skin stretched out between the base of his penis and groin.

"You've added an inch, one more. You can do it, sweetheart." Dr Fiona's encouragement was calm and measured.

Gemma repositioned her hands and recommenced pulling, harder this time. Pansy Paul shrieked again, it seemed more for show than any actual pain. Gemma pulled harder on his erection, it stretched more. Pansy Paul's face screwed up.

"I'd say that was six inches, sweetheart, nice job. A big increase in length. Temporary, of course." Dr Fiona giggled.

Gemma let go of Pansy's erection and he let out a gasp. Gemma knelt by him and stroked back a ponytail from his face. "My poor little

Pansy-puff. Don't worry." Her voice was soft and loving. "Would you like to do a cute cheerleader dance for Dr Fiona and Mr Jerome?"

He shook his head.

Gemma grabbed at his balls and put her hands around his balls. Pansy cried out, his voice high and hoarse at the threat of what her mischievous eyes told him "Tell me you want to do a cute cheerleader dance for us."

He shook his head with his eyes on Jerome.

She squeezed his balls, slow and hard. "No, don't." He nodded urgently, she let go and he closed his eyes.

She kissed one of his eyelids. "Good sissy, I knew you'd change your mind." She kissed the end of his nose with a feather-light touch. "You're my cute little pansy princess." She smiled sweetly at him "And don't forget to sing Dr Fiona's little songs." She cuddled him. "They are so funny."

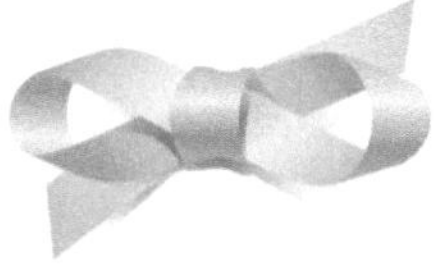

Chapter 3: Sissy Dance

D r Fiona sat next to Jerome and snuggled up to him on the sofa. She put her hands on her knees, waiting for the show with an expectant grin. Jerome fidgeted, unsure what to do about this bizarre situation. He had guessed he was a player in these two women's strange game.

Gemma stood over Pansy. She held his hands in the air. He held the two red pom-poms, the strips of material hanging loose over his fingers and his wife's. He tried to avoid looking at his assistant. His pleated dress hung flat and short against short bare legs. His tight top hugged his chest, a flabby chest clearly outlined. His former muscular pecs had gone. Dress straps stretched across his shoulders.

Dr Fiona crossed her legs, her little skirt across her thighs. "Let the dance begin," she said. She clapped a rapid rhythm, her smile wide and happy, teeth bright and perfect in the low light.

Gemma pulled Pansy into a dance, as if she were his puppet mistress. His face was flat and expressionless, his eyes dead and avoiding his assistant. Gemma made him wave the pom-poms high in the air as his dress flapped around his legs. It flowed up and down showing his red panties and the small outline of an erection.

Gemma and Dr Fiona burst into gales of laughter. Gemma doubled up in hysterics as she held his arms up. Jerome looked on and back at the two laughing ladies. He couldn't comprehend the scene unfolding in front of him. Pansy stopped dancing.

"Keep going, Princess, you look adorable," Gemma said between gulps of laughter. She shook his hands up. "You're such a wonderful sissy femboy prancing around like a girly cheerleader. Wiggle your bottom more, like a real cheerleader, not just a flabby sissy."

Pansy took up his bouncing dance again, hopping from foot to foot. He waved the pom-poms, his ponytails flicked from side to side and his skirt flapped around his thighs.

"And where's my song, Pansy the sissy cheerleader?" Dr Fiona said.

Pansy slowed a moment. He opened his mouth. "*I am a girly cheerleader, a pansy I've become, I want to suck off pretty sissies and swallow all their cum.*"

The two ladies erupted into gales of laughter. Jerome's jaw dropped open like a ventriloquist's dummy.

"*I am a girly cheerleader, a pansy I've become. I want to suck off sissies and swallow all their cum.*" Pansy hopped from foot to foot.

Gemma and Dr Fiona fell into more howls of laughter and Dr Fiona slapped her lap. Gemma pulled Pansy's flagging arms up high.

"*I am a girly cheerleader, a pansy I've become, I want to suck off sissies and swallow all their cum.*" Pansy's voice sounded distracted.

Gemma left Pansy and sat next to Jerome. She put her hand onto his lap. He froze and looked at his boss. Pansy's eyes shot to her hand hovering near his assistant's crotch.

Gemma unzipped Jerome's flies with one hand. He sat back with a start, his eyes meeting Pansy's. He looked back down again at Gemma's hand. She reached in and groped inside. Her face lit up and she pulled out Jerome's cock, big, black and hard. She wrapped her hand around it with a look of wonder. Jerome tried to move back but had nowhere to go. Pansy stopped dancing.

Dr Fiona got up and walked up to Pansy. She grabbed him around his neck and pulled his head down. She tucked him in a headlock with a crooked arm across her stomach. She put her other hand under his dress. She grabbed his balls hard, pulling them back. She had them with the grip of a vice and he dropped his pom-poms.

She pulled him to face Jerome. Gemma slid down onto the floor and between Jerome's legs. She grabbed at his trousers. And pulled them down with urgency, her mouth open, her tongue lolling. Sexual desire glowed in her face. She pulled Jerome's trousers and underpants to his ankles and over his shoes and socks. She threw them across the floor and turned back to face his gigantic cock. It stood bold, erect and enormous like polished coal. Dr Fiona pulled Pansy around to get a better view.

Gemma took Jerome's cock in one hand and she put her mouth over it greedily. Jerome's eyes shot to Pansy's again. Pansy looked away. Gemma's mouth went all the way down over the massive erection, She moved her mouth up and down, her lips sliding over its hard black surface. Jerome's eyes rolled, no longer thinking of his sissified boss.

Gemma stopped and stood, leaving Jerome on the edge. His huge erection quivered and a light drip of pre-cum on the tip glistened. Gemma put her hands under her dress and pulled her panties down and off.

Pansy must have guessed what was going to happen next. "No," he squealed, his voice trailing off to a plaintive, "*Ooooooooo.*" The sobs came after, "*Waaaaaaaaaaah.*"

Dr Fiona squeezed his balls harder. He squealed and snorted between sobs.

Gemma lifted her dress to her waist and held it there with one arm, her light patterned elastic stocking tops exposed. She climbed onto the sofa and mounted Jerome's raging cock. She wriggled her hips and slid down his greasy black pole. Her bare bottom faced Dr Fiona and Pansy as she pushed it towards them.

Pansy melted into tears that welled in his eyes. "*Waaaaaaaaaaaaah.*"

Gemma bounced up and down, impaled on Pansy's assistant's giant erection. Faster and faster she bounced, throwing her thick blond hair back and putting her arms under it. She groaned, "*Ooooh, ahhhhh.*" She fell forward onto Jerome's face, snogging him passionately. Her lips attached to his like a vacuum press. She swept her hands over his shaved head, his ears and his neck with passion. Her tongue wiped around his huge mouth as her bottom rose and fell like a storm wave against his erection.

Jerome groaned in sexual ecstasy. Gemma groaned and then screamed out as they held each other tight and orgasmed together. They froze at that the moment, grasping each other. Jerome gave out a growl like deep thunder and he jerked several more times as he ejaculated inside Gemma.

Pansy wailed at his wife having passionate sex in front of him with his assistant. Not just the humiliation of her having sex with another man, but one who was his underling at work.

Gemma flopped against Jerome, his giant cock fell out of her vagina and flopped against his bare leg. Gemma fell to one side, sitting next to Jerome, her legs wide open, her dress around her waist. Long drips of cum oozed out from her open damp vagina and onto the sofa.

"Clean up time, Pansy Princess." Dr Fiona said as Gemma closed her eyes and drifted into a doze, a light smile of pure satisfaction on her face.

Jerome laid back against the sofa, his eyes half shut. Dr Fiona pulled Pansy in the headlock and pushed his face towards Jerome's flaccid cock. Pansy recoiled, his nose creased up in disgust.

Fiona passed him a wet wipe. "Clean it up, sissy."

Jerome sat back but didn't push Pansy away, he seemed too satisfied to bother. Fiona held Pansy down. He faced his assistant's cock, a cock that had just cum inside his wife.

"Wipe Mr Jerome's man juices away like a good pansy boy." She pushed Pansy's hand onto the large penis.

Pansy held his assistant's limp cock with one hand with his face screwed up. He wiped away the remnants of cum around the end, his face twisted and screwed.

Gemma flicked her eyes wide and pulled her dress over her legs as she watched in fascination.

"What an adorable pansy you are." Dr Fiona said. "Now you can see what your sexy wife saw in your assistant's *prodigious membrum virile of Brobdingnagian proportions.*"

The room was silent. "Membrum virile is Latin for the *male member*," Dr Fiona explained. "Penis, in other words. Did you not do Latin at school, Pansy? You should have gone to an all-girl's private school in England as I did."

She stroked his balls through his panties, a hand under his red cheerleader skirt. "You would have also learnt that Brobdingnagian was the land where everything is big. It's in Gulliver's Travels, Princess." Her hand continued to swirl over his balls and erection, tantalising, teasing. "But I guess literature is not your thing. As a prissy sissy, you're probably better off with magazines full of photos of hot naked men having sex with each other."

Pansy moaned as Dr Fiona rubbed him with her slim hand, whirling and playing with his genitals.

"So let me put it in a way even you would understand, sissy boy," said Dr Fiona. "Your assistant has what you do not. A real man's cock."

Chapter 4: The Day After The Night Before

"Did you sleep well, Pansy darling?"

Light streamed in through the thin curtains. It was morning. Pansy blinked in the light and the memories of seeing his wife have sex with his assistant shot into his mind. Gemma sat on Pansy's bed next to Dr Fiona. Fiona must have stayed overnight. Gemma slipped a hand under the bed covers and massaged Pansy's sissy balls lightly. Dr Fiona's hand was on Gemma's leg, rubbing up and down. A white designer handbag lay by her other hand.

Gemma helped Pansy up and out of bed. He stood head bowed in bare feet as Gemma's hand swirled over his chastity cage, her fingers tucking under his sissy balls. His see-through pink baby-doll nighties hung on thin straps over his shoulders. It fluttered around the top of his erection. His eyes were watery and red. Gemma had woken him early after their late-night activities.

"We need to get you dressed for work, Pansy honey," Gemma said.

Dr Fiona put her hand under his wife's light blue dress as she took her husband's nightie off and placed it on his pink cartoon princess pillow. Gemma's eyes glowed with the attention from Dr Fiona's hand on her vagina. Her eyes met Dr Fiona's. Her eyes shifted to her hand over Pansy's penis cage. She shook it and pulled him towards her.

"How's your cute *Miss Clitty* this morning, little girl?" Gemma said, giggling. Dr Fiona rested her head on Gemma's shoulder, her stare was on Pansy's cage and her hand remained under Gemma's skirt.

Gemma stretched out his girly balls with her spayed fingers. "It's like a pretty tiny flower."

Gemma and Dr Fiona chuckled. She nuzzled Gemma's neck, but her eyes remained fixed on Pansy. "Her stretched-out girly balls look like two little wings," said Dr Fiona. "How about we call it her *little butterfly?*"

The ladies laughed. Gemma searched in her handbag and took out a small pink ribbon. She tied it around his balls and the back of his cage.

Dr Fiona looked at Pansy's decorated little sissy balls. "Maybe we could call it *Princess Pee Pee?*"

They laughed while Gemma adjusted the bow. Gemma went to her handbag. She pulled out small pink panties and held them up and stretched them out. The front had a long satin frill at the front. "Or maybe we should call it *Little Miss Kitty?*"

The ladies smirked.

"Put your foot up, cute little girl," said Gemma with a soft tone. She put the panties over one of Pansy's feet, then over the other. She slid them up his legs and over his balls and cage. She dug her hand inside the panties and his erection and balls and cage fell through the front. They were crotchless panties. The frill was like a sissy picture frame. The bow Gemma had tied lay across the front.

Gemma got a pair of dark stockings and a black suspender belt from the small wardrobe. Gemma turned Pansy to face her. She looked down at him, leaned down and kissed his cheek. "You make such an adorable little girl, I should have done this when we first met." She held his little penis. "*Little Miss Clitty* was never much use to me. Or should that be *Princess Pee-Pee?*"

Gemma took the suspender belt and hooked it around his chubby waist. She stroked his girly balls. "You're going to be such an adorable chubby little girl, I can't wait." She hunched her shoulders to her ears and kissed him hard full on the lips. Gemma lifted one of Pansy's feet. Pansy was still sleepy. Gemma rolled up the fine black stockings and slipped them over one foot then the other. She rolled them up his legs and clipped them to the suspender straps.

Gemma went back to the wardrobe and took out a pink satin bra. She did it up around the passive Pansy and put her hands to cup his chest. "Oh Pansy-boy, you're going to have a bust that will fit well in this pretty bra." She looked at Dr Fiona. "We need to start on her new diet and think about implants."

Pansy looked to the floor and then up again as her words sunk in. "Are you teasing?"

Gemma ignored him. "Your business suit is downstairs. You can put it over your pretty lingerie, Pansy Princess."

Pansy looked up. "I'm sure the outline of the bra and stocking straps will show."

Gemma caressed his girly balls, poking out from the panties. "I hope so, Pansy Petal. How else will anyone know you're a prissy pansy if they don't show through?"

Dr Fiona held up her phone. She flicked through the screenshots, photos of him from last night. They showed Jerome's cock in his wife's mouth and her making love with him sitting on his lap. Pansy's throat caught as she then scrolled through photos of him cleaning his assistant's massive cock.

Gemma took Pansy's hand. "Let's go downstairs, Princess, Mr Jerome is waiting to drive you to work. He stayed over last night and gave me another fantastic seeing-to. We had hot sex again. I have no idea why I spent all that time putting up with your ridiculous little thing."

They walked to the bedroom door hand in hand, Pansy in pink lingerie and stockings. Gemma stopped at the door. She took his balls and slithered her hand over them.

Pansy suddenly said. "Please can I cum now? It's been a long time."

Gemma laughed out loud. "Oh, Pansy Girl. Don't be ridiculous, of course you can't cum." She shook her head at Dr Fiona. "Don't forget, Pansy Princess. We have the photos and videos of you holding and cleaning Jerome's cock last night. So, I suggest you be a good girl today, otherwise we will have to use the photos."

"Use them for what?" Pansy looked horrified.

Gemma tickled under Pansy's girly balls for a moment, feeling the smooth skin. He giggled in a silly embarrassed way. She liked that. "If you're not a good girl, I'll post the photos online, of course, Pansy Princess. For everyone to laugh at you."

Chapter 5: Rivals

Robert Benedict walked into his office, ducking by habit as he passed through the door frame. He was an inch shorter than the height of the frame and his thick swept-back black hair brushed against it. He didn't want to risk putting his sculptured hair out of place. He'd spent ages moulding it into shape with gel that morning.

Robert looked out across the city from his top-floor office window. He stroked the ends of his thick moustache. The morning sky was red and the river choppy. His eyes settled on the black-glass building on the other side of the river. His eyes narrowed although his Botox smooth forehead remained smooth. The sign on the top of the building read Cochin Inc. Cochin, the company run by his fiercest business rival: Paul Paige.

He threw himself down in the high-backed black leather chair and he swivelled to look out on the cityscape again. Cochin Inc. and little Paul Paige. He thumped the top of the heavy dark-wood desk. The black wireless mouse jumped and landed back upright on the desktop.

Robert opened the report lying on his desktop: *3rd QUARTER FINANCE REPORT, ROBBEN CORP*. His Finance Director, John Swayner, had presented it earlier at the board meeting. He had bawled him out big time. He snarled at the thought. Swayner was just the messenger but who cares? Someone had to take the rap for the contents. Swayner was the perfect target. A soft wimp.

He pulled on the belt of his trousers. The belt dug into his belly and his stomach fell over it. He loosened it a notch, undid the top button and breathed out as if he'd been holding his breath.

He glared at the graph on page six of the report: ***Results comparisons: Cochin Inc. vs Robben Corp.*** His teeth gritted together; it was the screeching sound of chalk on a blackboard. The graph showed Cochin's sales overtaking his company and then outstripping Robben by 20% from January to October 2020. How had that happened? Robert threw the report across the room and it flapped against the wall. The pages flicked together and rested on the floor. It fell open on page six as if taunting him.

If losing market share wasn't bad enough, losing it to little Paul Paige's company was the worst. They had once been acquaintances; friends was too strong a word. But they had got along well enough. Robert stamped his foot at the memories and jarred his knee. He rubbed it, wondering if he was too competitive. Yes, of course he was, that's what made him a successful CEO and why he'd turn things around. He wasn't going to let little Paulie beat him, oh no.

He scowled. Little Paul Paige with his beautiful sexy wife. How did that little runt of a man get such a stunning wife? What was Paige, 5ft 6ins? What kind of height was that? A girl's height, that's what.

And there were those rumours he had a tiny dick. Yes, Paige's wife had to be in it for the money. What else could she want him for? Gemma needed a real man, someone like him, money and bags of macho testosterone.

He got up from his desk, walked to the large window and put his face against it. The neon-lit sign on the top of the building in the distance flickered through the light drizzling rain. The words taunted him: **Cochin Inc.** Robert imagined that arrogant little shit Paul Paige sitting there with his feet on his desk, flexing his fingers and discussing his own financial report. He imagined the broad smirk on little Paulie's face, telling his FD how he had beaten Robert Benedict. Paige, with the supermodel wife, Gemma. He glowered. It was unjust.

He slapped the window and it shook like a board. But what could he do to get revenge on little Paulie? How could he take him down? There had to be something. He shook his head, he had no ideas. He smiled broadly after a few moments, realising it didn't matter because something would come up. It always did. He needed to spot the opportunity when it arose and swoop to take Little Paulie down. He, Robert Benedict, CEO of Robben Corp, needed to show patience. It was only a matter of time.

Chapter 6: The Plan

Gemma sat relaxing in an armchair in the large living room. The early afternoon light was grey and flecks of snow drifted past the window. She was refreshed from the shower after her two-hour gym session in the basement.

She wore a short white ra-ra skirt and a tight top. She never used to wear such short skirts or tight tops, always preferring something more elegant. Now she loved sexy revealing clothes. It was something Karlene had taught her and now Dr Fiona encouraged too. It made sissies more desperate. Sissies were driven by appearances and sex, it was that simple. Wear something sexually enticing and you are halfway to controlling them.

Pansy was at the office and would be back early evening. She didn't allow him to go to the gym any more. Dr Fiona had advised that they'll fatten him up more at her school for behavioural change. The plan was to change into a cuter, more cuddly sissy femboy. Gemma liked that plan; her cute Pansy Princess would become a rounded little girly femboy. How divine, as Fiona would have said.

Gemma picked up her phone and typed a text message to Pansy. *"I hope you're being a good little girl today, darling Pansy."* She pressed send and it went off with a woosh.

Her phone pinged. *"Please Gemma, I'm in an important meeting."*

She typed back. *"You'll call me Goddess, Pansy. And then you'll tell me that you love being a sissy femboy for me."*

Ping. *"Sorry Goddess, give me 20 mins. I have to finish this meeting."*

Gemma typed. *"Type that now, girly-boy or I'll send out Dr Fiona's photos and videos of you."*

Ping. "I'm sorry Goddess, I love being your sissy femboy."

She typed, *"Good girl, that's better. Now cancel all your meetings for tomorrow because you're going to Dr Fiona's Institute. She, and her teachers, will train you to do sissy girly workouts. We're re-sculpting your body to be more appropriate for a tubby little sissy femboy who loves cock."*

Ping: *"OK, Goddess. Thank you, Goddess."*

Gemma put the phone down next to her. She had left strict instructions for Jerome. He was to bring Pansy home immediately after work and ensure he didn't exercise. Jerome had to provide Pansy with his food and drink at work. Gemma had given him the details of Pansy's new high carbohydrate diet. Pansy had to gain some girly fat to bulk up her bottom and chest. No more boyish muscular body shape, she wanted Pansy with tubby curves.

Jerome was also under instruction to watch over his sissy boss when he went to the toilet. She told Jerome to make sure her little girl of a husband used the bathroom like a sissy pansy and not a man. Pansy had to sit down in the toilet and never stand up. She told Jerome he had to stand in front of Pansy with the toilet door open.

She glanced outside aware of a permanent grin on her face. This was going well. Snow fell in breezy wisps and melted against the road surfaces. The tips of the grass were white. Gemma cradled a white china mug of green tea in both hands. Her mobile phone rang at that moment. It said Fiona on the screen. Gemma put her cup down, picked her phone up and tucked it under her blond hair to one ear. It clicked against her long pearl earrings. "Hello, Fiona."

"Gemma, Sweetheart." Fiona's deep creamy voice soared from the phone speaker like thick rich honey. "I've been thinking," she said, without preamble. "What you need is a wealthy man with an enormous phallus. That would be so divine. Jerome is good for humiliating Pansy, but he's not rich yet."

Gemma's face creased into a smile. She liked Fiona's no-nonsense approach. "I certainly enjoyed Jerome's enormous cock last night," she said not able to find it in her to copy Fiona's use of Latin. She then worried at the use of the slightly vulgar word *cock* when speaking with this sophisticated lady.

"Jerome was good for a bit of fun, Gemma sweetheart. However, a Goddess like you deserves so much more than just a well-hung hunk like Jerome. Although there's nothing wrong with tasting young stallions now and again." Fiona took a breath. "So, I have a proposal for you, I'm confident you are going to love it, sweetheart. It is part of my package of measures that involve the transformation of your pansy husband into an adorable sissy."

"I'm all ears, Fiona." Gemma removed an earring, shifted her phone to the other hand and settled into the sofa.

"Well, sweetheart, I'm certain you've heard of Mr Robert Benedict."

Gemma sat back up. "Yes, of course. And?"

"I am a friend and confidante of one of Robert's former girlfriends, Amanda Drummond-Smythe. She's a pretty girl and comes from a minor aristocratic British family. Small brain, big tits and a big mouth after a few glasses of Bollinger. You know the type of girl. A laugh like a horse."

Gemma didn't know that type of girl at all, but she mumbled, "*Yes.*"

"Well, sweetheart, Amanda told me something very interesting. Robert Benedict is...," Fiona adopted a lower conspiratorial tone and Gemma pushed the phone harder into her ear, "according to Amanda Drummond-Smythe, endowed with the most incredible twelve-inch cock. When fully aroused, of course. Not that I would know, of course, I merely repeat what I have been told."

Gemma frowned. "Yes," she replied with an inquisitive tone.

"Amanda says his testicles are a sight to behold: large, round and pendulous. She describes his bedroom skills as the most amazing she's ever experienced, he can last for ages. Apparently. Anyway, that's what Amanda says. Don't you think that is all rather delightful? Divine even."

"I guess so, Fiona," Gemma said. "But what's that got to do with me? Mr Benedict is my husband's fiercest business rival."

"Yes, sweetheart, I know. That's the point. Isn't that divine? Cuckolding Pansy with his biggest rival." Dr Fiona paused. "Through Ms Drummond-Smythe, I can introduce you to the extremely wealthy, well-hung Robert Benedict with his twelve-inch erection and exquisite bedroom abilities. He is single and he will adore you, who wouldn't? It's in the bag, so to speak."

"OK," said Gemma, not fully convinced. Wealthy and a big cock were good. On the negative side, she had heard that Benedict was arrogant and narcissistic.

Fiona said "I can hear by your voice you need convincing that this is the best for you. I believe it is an important step in turning your husband into the sissy femboy you want him to be. So what could be better for your husband's development and his transformation into a worthless sissy slut than to cuckold him with his biggest rival? It's simply divine, sweetheart." She took another pause to allow Gemma to take it in. Fiona then continued. "I'll arrange, through Ms Drummond-Smythe, for Robert to come here and you can see for yourself how amazing he is. When he's here, Pansy Princess will be your compliant little submissive sissy femboy, your pansy cuckold and sweet gay princess. She will sleep in her pink gay room."

"I suppose I could give him a try," Gemma said.

"Excellent, that's divine. I'll arrange it. I'll try for tonight. Strike while the iron's hot and all that. I'm sure Robert will jump at the opportunity to meet you, the stunning sexy Goddess wife of little girl Pansy Princess. You're reputation as the hottest wife in the city is assured and well-known, sweetheart."

"Meet him tonight, Fiona?"

"Yes, sweetheart. We'll prepare Pansy Princess before Robert arrives. Amanda told me that while Robert is macho with an ego the size of the Atlantic Ocean, he's a great lover so it's worth that little irritation. Remember Sweetheart, it was your idea to come to me to help you sissify and turn your husband into a sweet cuckold princess?"

Gemma felt warm, there was a tug of doubt but also a tingle of excitement in her gut. "OK, Fiona. I guess."

Dr Fiona had more. "And I'll have a little surprise for you."

Gemma sat up, interested. She liked surprises. "Do tell, Fiona."

"All will be revealed tonight." Fiona hung up.

Chapter 7: Housemaid

Gemma heard the front door open from the living room where she was listening to music; Pansy and Jerome were home from the office. She had laid out a short pink maid's dress next to her. The dress had several layers of pink petticoats and there was a small white apron with a white edge frill beside it. A pair of slim white shoes sat on the floor with high thin heels.

"In here, my darling," Gemma called out to Pansy. Her voice was soft and silky and a tingle of excitement crackled.

Pansy walked in with his head down. He approached Gemma. Jerome lumbered in after him, towering over his boss. Gemma hugged her husband, pulling him into her chest. She kissed him passionately with a closed mouth for several minutes, her fingers running through his long hair.

Gemma stopped. "Has she been a good sissy today, Jerome?"

"Yes, Ms Gemma." Jerome's voice was deep and bassy.

"And has she eaten lots of carbs?"

Jerome nodded and Pansy blushed deep red.

"Let's get you out of that nasty man suit and into proper sissy femboy clothing. I want you looking like an adorable little sissy slut again."

Pansy's head sunk into his shoulders.

"You can leave us now, Jerome. Thank you," Pansy said.

"No, Jerome," Gemma said sweetly. "I want you to stay and watch to see how much of a sissy princess your so-called boss is."

Pansy wanted to speak but thought better of it. His body slumped at the inevitable approaching humiliation. Gemma got up and walked around him, looking him up and down. "What a short little girly you are.

I'm going to put you in a pretty housemaid's dress with lots of frills and pink. You will look adorable and pretty, like a good little girly femboy should look." She lifted his hair and dropped it. "I'm going to curl the ends, it's too straight. I want your hair girly and pretty." She lifted the ends of his brown hair again and gave it some thought.

Gemma removed Pansy's suit jacket and passed it to Jerome who laid it over his arm. Pansy looked away, his eyes watering at the thought of the upcoming humiliation. His eyes fell on the frilly maid's dress and he swallowed hard.

Gemma towered over Pansy in her high heels. Her long bare legs were impossibly long and sensual below her tiny ra-ra skirt. She saw him drooling over her appearance; Fiona had been right. She touched the back of Pansy's head and pulled his head into her breasts. Her white satin blouse was tight and unbuttoned low. One of her bare smooth knees rubbed his thigh. She popped open Pansy's top shirt button followed by the others, one by one. The front opened revealing his white lacy bra underneath. She pulled the shirt off his arms and passed it to Jerome.

She got onto her haunches and removed his shoes and socks. With a sexy smirk, she undid his trousers and let them fall to the floor. Pansy stood in small frilly white panties. She spotted the tell-tale little erection bump at the front. He may look horrified, she thought, but somewhere deep inside, he was enjoying every moment of this. He enjoyed being her little girly sissy and this made her happy. She stroked his sissy balls through his panties for a few moments then planted a slow kiss on them.

She made him step out of the trousers by lifting his legs. She picked the trousers up, shook them flat and passed them to the waiting Jerome. She placed her hand flat against his small erection. She felt the soft light material of his little panties and pressed against his erection.

"You're so pretty in this enchanting pretty lingerie, my darling little girl. What do you think, Jerome?"

Jerome looked to the floor and mumbled something indistinguishable.

Gemma swirled her hand over Pansy's erection. "I can feel that little *Miss Clitty* is excited at the prospect of you being dressed in pretty sissy clothing again."

Gemma got up and picked up the frilly pink dress. She tugged it over Pansy's head and pulled it tight over him. She stepped back to admire it. Her deep blue eyes sparkled, a captivating smile teasing her lips. Pansy's dress was wide, flaring from his waist, a single pink satin film sat over layers and layers of pink chiffon frills. They bundled around the top of his thighs. His sleeves were puffed out high on his arms, tight against his arms.

Gemma held her hands together. "Oh Pansy, you're adorable, such a cute sissy princess." She took both his hands and held them out, grinning broadly. She looked at him for a few moments and then pushed his feet into the high heels. She stood back and looked Pansy over again and pulled a face; something wasn't right. She thought for a moment then nodded. She tugged at his panties, visible under the layers of frills.

She knelt down and without warning, pulled his panties to his ankles and off his feet over his shoes. He tottered on his heels. "Little *Miss Clitty* is as hard as a little nail." She tweaked it for several moments. It was ruining the look. She retrieved one of two pink ribbons from the sofa. She bent over and looped the ribbon around the back of his small balls. She tied them and pulled the ribbon tight on the top of his balls at the base of his little erection. She pulled tighter still and looped the ribbon into two bows.

She nodded to herself, "That looks much prettier. You look adorable with a cute little girly clitty."

She ran a finger under the end of his erection. Pansy's flushed red and he closed his eyes. She rubbed the end of his erection, pulling back the skin and massaging the little slit at the end. "Now I'm going to do something different in your hair, Pansy." She looked to Jerome standing still and not knowing what to do. "Keep an eye on her while I get the curling tongs."

Pansy's eyes shot to her. "Curls?"

She rubbed his cheek with one hand while stroking the end of his erection. "Of course, sweet cake. You want to look pretty for me, don't you?" Gemma left the room and returned minutes later with back curling tongs and a circular wooden hairbrush. She plugged the tongs in next to her armchair. "Sit down, Pansy Princess." She placed her hands on Pansy's head and he slumped into the chair. She touched the curling tongs quickly. They were hot.

Pansy had worn his hair brushed back from his face to the office. It was straight back on the top of his head and away from his face at the sides and across his ears. It wasn't feminine enough for her. Gemma brushed Pansy's dark-brown hair straight down down to his shoulders. A smile creased over her face seeing it longer and more feminine. She brushed it forward over his eyebrows and left it that way. He blinked as it tickled his eyelashes.

She inserted the tongs into the bottom of his hair and curled it up. She waited a few moments until the bleeper sounded. The smell of slightly singed hair wafted up. She took the tongs away and squealed with excitement. The ends were curled up, resting on the top of his narrow shoulders.

Gemma continued curling the ends of his hair then stepped back to inspect it. Pansy had a fringe and pretty curls at the end of his hair. She put the tongs down and made a ponytail inside his hair at the back. She tied a pink ribbon in the back of his hair. She made two large bows, they were stiff and stood up above the top of his head.

She took his hand and guided him to stand and he balanced on his high heels. She grinned at him thinking he looked wonderful. Just below the line of petticoats, his little erection and balls were visible and the bow around them matched the bow in the back of his hair. She held up his balls in one hand. "Don't they look cute, Jerome?"

Jerome glanced at her, looked away and mumbled a yes, Ms Gemma without meaning it.

She turned back to Pansy. "I wonder what Robert Benedict would say if he saw you now, darling princess?"

Pansy woke out of his moodiness. "Why would you say that, Goddess?" His voice wavered. "That's a step too far to even think that. He's a horrible man."

Gemma wrapped her hands around his pussy balls, swirling and massaging them with her soft gentle touch. She watched her hands as she moved them. "I just wondered what the tall, masculine Mr Benedict would think seeing his business rival looking like you do now. You're sissy, cute and pretty in your pink housemaid's dress. I'm sure he would adore seeing your girly hairstyle and your tiny *Miss Clitty* on show with a pink ribbon on it." Her hand brushed around his pussy balls.

Pansy pulled a hard face. "I'd prefer not to think about *him*." He spat out the pronoun.

"Poor Pansy," Gemma said softly. She continued to rub his balls and then squeezed a little. "Princess Peewee, you will have to think of Mr Benedict. You're a little gay sissy and gay siss girls love big macho men like Mr Benedict." Her voice was calm and soft.

Gemma pushed up against Pansy, her hand still clamped around his little balls. She kneaded his balls like two small dough balls. "She kissed him, sucking on his lip. Then she squeezed his balls harder, her hand taut and firm.

Pansy's watered up.

Gemma loosened her grip and he breathed out after expecting her to squeeze harder. She brushed her lips against his then kissed him harder, passionately. He relaxed.

"What would Robert Benedict say if he saw you in this pretty sissy dress, Pansy Princess?"

He looked up at her, tears welled in his eyes at the horror of the thought.

"I think Mr Benedict would love to see you like this, don't you? Seeing you, his rival, dressed as an adorable little sissy, squealing like a pansy girl?"

Pansy shook his head. "Why do you keep talking about him?"

Gemma moved away, a serious expression on her face. "Wait there while I get ready, Pansy. I have a hot date with a new hot man this evening so I need to put on a sexy dress and beautiful makeup."

Pansy moved towards her, he put out a hand and tried to touch her breasts. She slapped him away. His hand moved to her bottom under her little skirt. She pulled his hand away, a smile stuck on her lips.

"Please don't go on a date, Goddess," he said. "I'll do whatever you tell me, I'll wear whatever you say. Please, not again. I can't stand it." He sniffed a sob.

"You're so sweet when you weep. Such a sweet sissy femboy." Gemma said kindly. She turned to Jerome, waiting by the door, his hands clasped in front of his body. "Make sure Pansy waits here like a good little girl. I'm going upstairs to get ready." Gemma raised her wrist to look at her jewel-encrusted watch. "They'll be here in thirty minutes. Got to rush."

"They?" Pansy asked. "Who'll be here?"

Gemma took Pansy's erection between her fingers and rolled it absent-mindedly. Pansy gasped and his breathing increased. Gemma ran her fingernails over his little pussy balls and up and down his tiny penis. Her hand rolled on his balls. "You'll be finding out in thirty minutes, little girl. There is one thing I will tell you though." Gemma considered his balls and compressed them lightly with her fingertips several times. She seemed absorbed.

"What will you tell me?" Pansy asked.

Gemma's lips grinned with a thin closed smile. "I can tell you that they're going to adore you."

Chapter 8: A New Boyfriend

THE WALL CLOCK TICKED down the minutes while Pansy waited in the living room with deep worries about what his wife had planned. His eyes caught Jerome's and they looked away simultaneously. Neither had got used to this new reality, it was too weird.

Jerome said, "Erm, I need to check on the food." He left and they were both pleased to be alone for a while, Jerome returned from the kitchen. Gemma had asked him to prepare dinner for her guests. Pansy hadn't known that his assistant could cook, he was a man of many talents and Pansy immediately thought of the talent for screwing his wife and felt hot with jealousy.

The smell of roast chicken took his mind away fork the image. Jerome stood in the living room and clasped his hands in front of his body, looking like a nightclub bouncer. How had it come to this? His personal assistant now followed his wife's orders rather than his.

Pansy rested his hands on his bare legs. A cool breeze from somewhere blew around his erection and little balls. The layers of pink petticoat that framed his small genitals felt like an elaborate picture frame. He tried to pull the petticoats over his erection but they were too short and stiff and he only attracted the attention of his assistant. Jerome looked at his erection for several moments too long for comfort. He suddenly realised and flung his stare into a distant focus and they both sighed in relief. The wit was terrible.

The sound of sharp footsteps descending the stairs told them of Gemma's imminent arrival. She breezed into the living area, her hips swinging as if she were on the modelling catwalk again. The scent of her rich perfume overpowered the heavy smell of chicken. Gemma's white cocktail dress shimmied and swayed like a flag in a gentle wind. A wide frill ran around the bottom of her dress and around the long split which flowed up one side to the top of her thigh. Pansy gasped at how beautiful she was.

Gemma stopped and put one leg forward. The long split in her dress fell on either side of her long defined never-ending limb. Her smooth stockings glittered in the room lighting. Her white shoes were slim and high. A single wide shoulder strap went from her wide shoulder and across her 36DD breasts. The other shoulder was exposed and her blond hair curled into her round blooming cheeks and over her shoulder. Her lips were plumped with bright red lipstick and her large blue eyes outlined in dark eyeliner and misty-grey eyeshadow.

Pansy's eyes bulged at the sight of his hot sexy wife. He wanted her and stood and went up to her. He put his hands around her and cuddled his head into her breasts. Gemma put her hands behind her, untwisted his arms and put them at his sides. She kissed him on the forehead. He pushed one hand towards one of her boobs. She kept her lips on his and slapped his hand away. He put a hand on her exposed thigh and she moved that away with a smile and a gentle shake of her head. "No touching, Pansy. You're my gay sissy femboy submissive, not a heterosexual husband." Her tone was gentle and loving.

Pansy's lips pursed. "But you look so stunning, so hot and sexy. I want to hold you and make love to you. You're my wife when all is said and done."

Gemma took his hands and pushed her leg out further. Pansy's eyes flowed over it. "Yes, you're my husband but that doesn't mean we'll have sex. You're a sissy pansy so no touching Goddess. I have a hot date tonight and I want to look good for him and I don't want my hair messed up."

Pansy put his hands together as if in prayer, he swallowed, his mouth was dry. "Please, please. Don't do this again."

A chime rang out around the hall cutting him short. It echoed to a still silence.

"My guests have arrived," Gemma said, turning to Jerome. "Be a good boy and let them in."

Pansy ran his hands over his maid's outfit and down over his little exposed erection. "They can't see me like this. My genitals are exposed under my petticoats."

Gemma hugged her cheek on his. "Yes, I know, Pansy. Thanks because you're a little sissy boy"

The bow on Pansy's sissy balls was large and tight, squeezing them. His eyes flitted around the room, looking for an escape. There was none. Pansy heard the front door open. Moments later, it closed. Dr Fiona's voice carried through although her words were indistinct. There were four pairs of footsteps, they got louder as they approached the living room, one was the sound of a female in heels. Two other pairs were both heavy and flat; hard leather on tiled floor. A fourth was light and also in heels. It seemed like there were two men and two women. Pansy wanted to flee but he had nowhere to go.

Jerome the room and stood back with his hands resting in his now familiar bouncer pose, clasped in front of his body. Dr Fiona followed him clad in a tight petrol-blue dress to her knee. Her long, almost black hair lay over one shoulder and down her front. Thin shoulder straps held up two V-shape pieces of dress which clung over her large breasts. Her elegant shoulders were bare. She strode to Gemma and kissed her on the lips and Pansy saw the back of her dress was open to her bottom. He saw a black tattoo of two wings from one slim hip to the other.

Fiona's dark-brown eyes roved over Pansy with satisfaction and settled on the bow around his little erection. "What happened to my curtsey, sissy?" she said.

Pansy tried to keep his tongue from lolling out of his mouth at the sight of Dr Fiona. He took the sides of his dress and dipped a curtsey. The two ladies giggled at the sight of his little erection and pussy balls poking from the pink petticoats.

Pansy looked at the door with impending doom. There had been two sets of male footsteps, one set was Jerome's. Whose did the other set belong to? And who was the other woman?

A small blond girl clicked into the room with long bog hair. Her makeup was overdone - she wore thick red lipstick, long black false eyelashes and dark lined eyebrows. Her heels were so high she was on tip-toes. Her breasts were bigger than Dr Fiona's and her skirt was pink and tiny. Her eyes were on the floor as she staggered into the room, finding it difficult on her heels.

"Pixie, how wonderful to see you again," said Gemma. "Pixie is the surprise?"

"Well, she will be the agent of the surprise, yes," said Fiona.

Gemma pursed her lips. Fiona could be obtuse at times but never mind, she had arranged a wonderful evening.

A long broad shadow fell into the living room from the hall. All eyes went back to the doorway. A tall wide-shouldered form filled the door frame and back-swept raven-black hair brushed against the top of the frame. The figure took two steps into the room, his dark blue jacket undone. A large stomach poured over a pulled black leather belt with a gold buckle.

Robert Benedict glared around the room. His eyes flowed over Pansy and his eyebrows raised an inch his gaze settled on Gemma. His face creased into a lecherous tight-lipped grin.

Chapter 9: Dinner Party

Pansy stepped back and bumped into Gemma. She held his shoulders. "Curtsey to Mr Benedict, Princess, and say, *hello Sir.*" She said with a hint of amusement in her voice.

Pansy looked back and up at his wife. "I will do no such thing?"

Benedict's head tilted, he recognised the voice but hadn't worked out it was his fiercest rival in the housemaid frills. His eyes fell on Pansy's exposed tiny erection beneath the layers of pink. Confusion swept through his eyes.

Gemma pushed her hand between Pansy's thighs and grabbed his balls. She squeezed hard. Pansy curtsied, his cheeks and neck glowed puce with anger as he said, "Hello Sir." His head felt as if it were about to explode. Benedict's eyes widened in shock, Dr Fiona hadn't explained the entire situation to him. She had only explained that Gemma wanted to meet him as her husband was unable to satisfy her in bed; an invitation he had cleared his evening diary for.

Gemma walked past Pansy, took his hand and walked up to Benedict. "Nice to meet you, Robert, Fiona has told me all about you." She looked down to the floor and flushed a little. "And about how well-endowed you are."

Benedict looked all over her as if his eyes were feasting on a rich meal. They kissed each other on the cheek and lingered a while, the kiss straying to the edge of their lips. Gemma flushed like a young girl as she looked up at the rugged Robert Benedict. He was 6ft 5ins of masculinity and testosterone. He looked back at her with desire smoking in his eyes. He hitched his belt up into his hanging stomach.

Gemma took his hand with her free hand. "Let's go to the dining room. Jerome has cooked chicken and vegetables and my sissy housemaid will be serving us."

"And Pixie," added Dr Fiona.

This was the first that Pansy had heard of this. His stomach rumbled at the thought of roast chicken.

"I know what you're thinking, Pansy." Dr Fiona said. "So I asked Jerome to prepare bread with lots of butter, fried potatoes and white pasta for you and a salad for Pixie." She grinned. "One sissy chubby and rounded, the other small and slim."

"I would like the chicken," Pansy said.

Fiona reached down and tickled under the head of his erection with a fingernail. "Don't be silly, Pansy. How can we fatten you up and give you a massive bottom if you eat chicken?"

They went to the dining room. Gemma and Fiona sat opposite each other at the head of the dark table. Benedict sat at Gemma's right hand. They banished Jerome to eat in the kitchen. Pansy watched with despair at Gemma and Benedict talking closely, their eyelashes batting in sync and their mouths uncomfortably close together.

Pansy and Pixie served the food, rushing to and from the kitchen, curtseying with each serving. Once served, Pansy and Pixie sat on chairs in the corner of the dining room chewing miserably on their food. Pansy struggled with the carbohydrate-heavy food but Dr Fiona had told him he had to eat everything. All of it. She said he was on a crash anti-diet and they all laughed.

Once they finished their meals, Pansy and Pixie brought in coffee for them, curtseying. Pansy was feeling bloated; Dr Fiona had made him eat far too much and too many refined carbohydrates. He didn't know how he had managed to swallow all that pasta. Dr Fiona forced him with a broad smile and a hand clamped around his balls. She tightened it every time he was too slow eating the portions.

Gemma took a sip of coffee and sat back. "So Robert, have you guessed who Pansy is yet?" Her large steel-blue eyes danced and glittered.

Benedict chortled a moment. "If I didn't know any better, I'd say that Pansy was Paul Paige. But it can't be. No man would have such a tiny dick and balls and they wouldn't be dressed as a little maid girl?" He chuckled again. "I guess you found a look-alike? She's a good likeness. Very amusing."

Gemma's face went serious. "Well, you see, Robert, that is precisely the problem. Pansy is indeed my husband Paul and her tiny little dick is the problem."

"What?" Benedict's mouth gaped open. He stared at Pansy and back at Gemma

Pansy felt his face burn with humiliation.

Gemma continued. "Since my husband has such a girly dick and pussy balls, the only sensible thing to do was to turn her into a sissy pansy. Fiona has helped me. And now I need to find a real man. Which is where you come in."

Benedict appraised Pansy from the table, he raised one eyebrow and nodded. He looked impressed at what they'd done to his rival. Gemma put her hand under the table and onto his leg. Benedict grinned and looked at Pansy again. Pansy looked away, he didn't want to see his rival with his wife. It hurt. But why was his penis so damn hard at the thought of it?

Dr Fiona spoke from the opposite end of the table. "Robert, darling, we're fattening Pansy up and we've changed her diet and turning her into a chubby little pansy princess. We're not only changing her personality and mannerisms, but we'll also be giving her a chubby little girl figure. She's going to look adorable when she becomes a corpulent little girl." Her eyes screwed up in a smile.

Benedict was taking all the new information in as Gemma pushed her hand up his leg. It met the end of his long cock through his trousers. She slipped her hand over it and she ran her fingers up and down its length. "This is a real man's cock, Robert, not like my little girly husband's girly clitty," she said.

They both looked at Pansy who looked away.

Gemma kissed Benedict hard. She forced her hand harder onto his cock and rubbed it up and down its length. It grew harder.

"Wow, Robert, it's true. You're a very big boy indeed," said Gemma. She pulled his neck with her other hand and locked her mouth tight on hers. She lashed her tongue into his mouth. Benedict responded and the two kissed deeply for several minutes. Dr Fiona watched them with satisfaction as she walked to Pansy and took his hand.

Gemma and Benedict stood together, snogging with desperate passion. Their hands moved over each other's bodies, Gemma pushed her fingers onto his cock through his trousers. Benedict put his hand to her breasts.

"No," said Pansy, watching the events with mounting horror.

Dr Fiona held Pansy's hand tighter. "*Shhh*, Pansy. Your wife has found a real man, let her get on with what nature intended. I want you to watch and enjoy."

Gemma pushed Benedict back over the dining table. She launched her hands at his trousers, ripping them down. It was as if her hands were a tangle as she pulled down his boxer shorts. She and Dr Fiona gasped when Benedict's huge twelve inches sprung into the cool dining room air.

Pansy stifled a, "No."

Dr Fiona pulled Pansy to the table by his hand, his head down. Benedict looked at him and smirked. She let go and passed Pansy's hand to Gemma. Gemma took Pansy's hand and pulled him to his knees with her so they kneeled side by side. She threw her other hand over Benedict's cock and squeezed Pansy's hand lovingly. He was about to get a close-up of his wife sucking on Benedict's dick. Gemma put her mouth over Benedict's huge cock with undisguised desperation. A cock-shaped lump stuck out from her cheek.

She circled her lips around his cock, sucking and slurping. She clawed at his giant balls with her hand, her other rubbing the back of Pansy's hand. She pushed her head further down his shaft. She swallowed it down her throat, her lips landing against her hand at the base of his erection.

A long "*Eeeeeeeeeeeek.*" sounded from Pansy next to her.

Gemma withdrew her mouth and made one more circling slurp on the end of Benedict's cock. She turned around and raised her skirt. She slipped down her panties with one hand and bent over, her ripe open vagina beckoned him. Her hand remained locked tightly in Pansy's hand.

"*Nooooooooooooo,*" squealed Pansy with a sob and a sniff. Pansy's shoulders heaved as he wept at the sight of his wife and bitter rival.

Gemma looked back at Benedict. "Do it, big boy. Now."

Benedict stood and took his twelve-inch rod in his right hand. He touched it to Gemma's inviting vagina. Her labia parted, damp and warm. He guided it to her and slid it in. He faced Pansy over Gemma's back and smirked again, his eyes narrowing. Gemma grunted, her eyes widened in shock, she had never felt such a size inside her. Dr Fiona gazed in wonder as it disappeared inside her. He pushed it up to the hilt as if putting a sword deep into a scabbard. He withdrew slowly, almost to the end then pushed it hard Then again. Faster this time, Faster harder. His body slapped against hers.

"Do it, lover. Do it. Fuck me. Harder, faster. Oh my god," she panted as Robert impaled her time and time again.

Gemma's head swayed and Pansy wailed in despair.

Dr Fiona encouraged them. "Robert, show Gemma what her husband could never give her."

They froze at that moment in shared orgasm and groaned in ecstasy. Benedict moved in and out a couple more times and stopped. The giant flaccid cock fell out of Gemma and he flopped against her back. She let herself down to the floor and they laid entwined together. Their breathing slowed to normal and the room returned to silence. The quiet was punctured by the ticks of the wall clock and Pansy's soft sniffles. Pansy wiped tears from his eyes. The torture was over, he hoped.

Dr Fiona called. "Pansy, I have a job for you now."

It seemed his humiliation was not over yet.

Chapter 10: Sissy Time

Pansy's lips were tight and down-turned as he cleaned his wife's open vagina with a wet wipe. He wiped away his rival Benedict's thick gloopy cum; with each wipe, more cum dripped out. Pansy sobbed silently as he cleaned. Dr Fiona stood by him, directing him with her hands on his. He finished and sat back with a mix of horror and a weird fascination at what had just happened.

"And now it's the Pansy and Pixie show," said Dr Fiona.

Benedict propped himself up on one elbow, his enormous soft penis hung low between his thighs. He caressed one of Gemma's nipples with a loose hand and a lopsided grin of gratification and confidence across his lips. All Pansy's business victories against him were now a long-distant memory, he had given retribution. Robert Benedict had cuckolded Pansy Paul Paige in front of his own eyes and he wallowed in the sense of a final victory. Nothing could be more victorious than publicly cuckolding your biggest rival.

Dr Fiona lined Pansy and Pixie up next to each other. She lifted Pixie's tiny skirt to her waist and pulled her panties to her knees. A large clitty stood out to attention as her eyes batted with fake embarrassment. Dr Fiona pushed Pansy's hands around the huge penis as Pixie continued to pretend to look shy and demure. The comparison with Pansy's petite girly dick was stark. Despite Pixie's small stature, her penis was around eight inches long and as stiff as a metal rod.

Pansy craved a release; he was bursting and tense with desperation. The desperation was made worse by the deep, familiar smell of his wife's sex, mingled with that of his rival's. He didn't understand how what he had witnessed could turn him on. He decided there must be something wrong with him.

Dr Fiona grabbed Pansy's ear and twisted him to his knees, facing Pixie's erection. Pixie put a hand to her mouth and sniggered at Pansy's little erection and pink bow which poked from below his short maid dress.

"You're going to use your mouth on pretty Pixie's stunning clitty," she said.

Pansy shook his head, pleading with his eyes. Benedict sat up, his eyes glinting at this latest humiliation for his rival. This was like all his Christmases at once.

Dr Fiona took Pansy's face in her hands and pushed his lips towards the end of Pixie's hard strong erect penis. She lifted Pixie's erection onto Pansy's lips. Pansy shivered and heard Benedict laugh. "She looks so cute with this on her lips," said Dr Fiona. "Pansy-Blowjob."

Gemma and Benedict laughed out loud.

Dr Fiona held Pansy's nostrils closed with her fingers and he opened his mouth to breathe. She guided his open mouth over the end of Pixie's erection. Pansy tried to pull his head away but Dr Fiona twisted his ear with a crack. She shoved his mouth fully over the erection and let go of his nose. A faint musky non-feminine smell flowed into his mouth and up his nostrils. He held back a choke. She pushed his lips over the end and he tasted salt and dampness. He shuddered again but the feeling of a mouth full of hard erection was more pleasing than he'd anticipated. That was odd.

"Deeper, sissy slut, all the way to your tonsils," Dr Fiona said with a gentle lilt in her voice.

Pixie's erection was warm on his tongue and it hardened further. Pansy shuddered and saw his wife turn onto one side to watch, her face more beaming and alive than he'd seen her for a long time. It made him happy to see her enjoying herself. Her eyes twinkled with mischief and her lips parted with sexual excitement at seeing him in this situation.

Pansy saw her large naked firm breasts with the dark nipples erect and proud. His throat caught. He wanted those nipples in his mouth. Pixie's smooth hard erection jerked in his mouth.

Dr Fiona maintained her hand on his ear. She twisted it almost in a full circle and forced his mouth down the shaft of Pixie's erection. Pixie was smooth and had a scent of perfume and moisturiser around her genitals. And a faint male musk. Pansy felt Pixie's veins stretch and pump against his tongue as the tip caressed his tonsils.

"Further Pansy-Blowjob, all the way in. Swallow up pretty Pixie's girly clitty like a good slutty pansy puff," Dr Fiona said.

"I love to see my little girl Pansy with a large object in her mouth," said Gemma. ."Her mouth was made for sissy clitty, don't you think Fiona?"

"Oh yes, sweetheart. Little Pansy-Blowjob was made to swallow sissy cum. Lots of it." Dr Fiona pulled Pansy's head up and down Pixie's erection. Pixie threw her head back and a low sound of pleasure came from her throat.

"Are you enjoying this, Pixie?" asked Gemma.

"Oh yes," she replied.

"Good," said Gemma. "Princess-Blowjob is the perfect sissy slut and she's going to learn to give great blowjobs." She pushed her face inches from Pansy's face. "Are you enjoying yourself, sissy slut?"

Pansy grunted in a reply that could have been yes or no. He was merely acknowledging his wife's question. Truth be told, he was loving and hating it at the same time.

Dr Fiona manoeuvred Pansy's head up and down by his ear, faster and faster, Pixie groaned in rhythm to Pansy's movements and moved her hips. Her huge erection filled his throat.

Pixie called out, *"Oh."*

Dr Fiona stopped. She pulled Pansy's mouth off Pixie's erection by his hair and turned him around. Pixie's smooth solid erection pulsed and throbbed on the point of cumming and her face was distraught with disappointment. Dr Fiona rammed Pansy's head facing downwards between her thighs with him on all fours. His flared petticoats formed a circle of frills around his exposed bottom and open sissy vagina. The ribbon was tight around the back of his girly balls.

Pixie gave a girly smile realising what Dr Fiona now had in mind and sat up onto his knees. Dr Fiona grabbed Pixie's stiff throbbing erection and pulled it towards Pansy's sissy vagina. Pixie didn't need to be persuaded as she knew what to do and had been well trained. Pixie pushed the end of her erect clitty against Pansy's hole. Pansy flinched. The huge end rested hard against his anus. Pixie shoved it harder but still it didn't enter.

"It's too big," squealed Pansy. "It won't fit." But he tingled in anticipation at the thought of what was to come. Sometimes, he pondered, you need to be shown new experiences to understand,

Dr Fiona reached down, grabbed his nose and twisted it. "Be quiet, sissy girl." She stood up and wiped cold gel around his sissy vagina.

Pixie breathed in deeply to compose and ready herself. She thrust her narrow hips firmly and her erection bowed an instant with the pressure against her new lover's sissy vagina. It hovered on the precipice and then disappeared inside with a pop. Pansy had relaxed and accepted his new experience. He gave out a huge groan of pleasure as Pixie's small smooth body slapped against his buttocks. A wide grin came over Pixie's face as she pulled back and thrust it in deep again; there was another slap of skin on his buttock cheeks. Pansy had never felt such wonderful sensations before. His entire sissy vagina seemed to light up with erotic electric feelings.

Pixie's face flushed red through her makeup as she thrust in several times more. Her hips moved back and forth and her erection slid in and out of Pansy's sissy vagina, moving more smoothly. Pansy wailed but not in pain as Pixie groaned and mumbled with delight. Gemma took one of Pansy's hands and rubbed it with her thumb, a look of love on her lips as Pixie had passionate sex with her husband.

Pixie thrust faster and her eyes rolled up. Pansy's wails and sexual groans continued as he seemed to find something new and exciting in what was happening. His face looked lost in sexual ecstasy. Then Pixie screamed out like a whip cracking and her thrusts slowed. She came to a rest and fell back. Her now flaccid clitty slid out of Pansy's anus and flopped against her leg. A single string of cum lined the route between Pansy's hole and the end of Pixie's limp clitty.

Gemma rubbed Pansy's cheek with a crooked finger. "I'm so proud of you, Pansy," she cooed. "You took that like a real slutty sissy." She beamed. "Your sissy virginity has been taken."

Dr Fiona kept Pansy in her thigh hold and looked over him to see gloops of Pixie's juice plop out of Pansy's sissy vagina drop by drop like a slow dripping tap. Pixie pulled her panties back up and sat in the corner looking satisfied and satiated.

"That was fun," said Dr Fiona. "And now, Pansy, you must show respect to your wife's new lover. You will address him as Mr Benedict and he will become the man of the house and you the sissy housemaid."

Tears welled in Pansy's eyes although he wasn't sure if that was his utter humiliation of the strange sense of excitement stirring in his stomach. Benedict lay naked next to Pansy's stunning naked wife and propped himself up on his elbows. He looked straight at Pansy and his teeth glinted in a wide smile and stroked his moustache like a cat wiping off the cream. He was a winner and he'd just won his rival's wife and humiliated him.

Chapter 11: Consummation

"It's time for your *beddy-byes*, little girly." Gemma spoke with a gentle motherly tone. She was still naked and Pansy gawked at her pert but large weighty breasts bouncing as she moved towards him. She took his erection in her hand. "Little *Miss Clitty* is still so hard. Would my little gay sissy boy like to cum? Would you like to spurt all over your Goddess's big firm breasts?"

She wiggled her tits side to side in his face. He nuzzled into them, closing his eyes in delight. He put a hand to her erect nipple. Gemma swiped his hand away and moved back. "No touching your Goddess, Pansy puff." Her voice was soft with the hint of a smile and she played with the end of his little erection, rolling it, rubbing, pushing his little foreskin up and down.

Pansy gasped, his face softened. He breathed out, "*Ahhhhhh.*"

Gemma pulled her fingers away. "Time to stop touching *Miss Clitty*, Pansy." She swiped at his erection and he recoiled. "My Pansy Princess's is not allowed to cum. No one wants to see your nasty sissy juices squirting all over the place, do they Sissy?" She leaned in and kissed him deeply and passionately for several seconds. Pansy looked up into her creased amused eyes. "I want to cum. I need to."

"Don't be ridiculous, Pansy," she replied. "I just told you. Little sissies mustn't make nasty sissy messes, it's disgusting. That's the end of the discussion and it's now bedtime for you. Little girls need their beauty sleep."

Benedict watched and listened to their conversation, a leer spread wide across his face. He had a hand on his giant cock and held it up towards Pansy, as if to say *look at a real man's cock.*

Gemma told Pansy to raise his arms. She grabbed his frilly dress and pulled it off over his head. She unclipped his bra and told him to remove his shoes. She untied the bow from his little penis and girly balls and the one at the back of his hair. Benedict continued to rub gently on his cock. It had become semi-hard again, the man was insatiable and his gaze fell on Gemma as he played with himself, as if he was thinking of her as he rubbed himself.

Pansy hadn't noticed that Dr Fiona had left the room until she breezed back in. She carried a pink baby-doll nightie and large pink panties. She passed the panties to Gemma who held them up to Pansy's face with a wide happy grin. His face dropped. The back of the panties had a message inscribed on them in dark pink writing – **PRINCESS.**

Gemma's eyes sparkled with fun. She bent and clipped on the cage that Fiona had brought in. She lifted one of Pansy's legs and slipped the panties over it, then the other. She pulled it up snugly over his erection. She spun him around to see how they looked on him. She was satisfied seeing the words written across Pansy's firm bottom. She pulled the baby-doll nightie over his head. "I want you to tell Mr Benedict how much you love being a pansy princess, how you love to play with other sissies and how you understand why he should have sex with me. And call him Sir."

Pansy hesitated. Gemma grabbed his sissy balls through his pink panties and pulled him towards Benedict. Pansy looked to the floor. "Now, sissy femboy." She held his hand, rubbing the back with her free hand while she squeezed his balls with the other hand.

Pansy sniffed and cleared his throat. Gemma squeezed his balls, digging her nails into the soft inner sacks to remind him what he had to say. Benedict leaned back and grinned, his moustache framed his large lips. Perfect white teeth glinted between the black whiskers.

Pansy looked to the floor. "I love being a pansy princess." Pansy's voice wobbled. "And playing with other sissies." The words caught in his throat. "And I understand you have to have sex with my wife, Sir"

Gemma clapped her hands. "What an adorable little girl you are, Pansy. I'm so proud of how you are." She took Pansy's hand and led him to the door to the hall. She turned back. "Robert, meet me in the master bedroom. Don't bother getting dressed, I haven't finished with you." Her eyes flowed over his huge erect cock. "I see you're ready for me too."

She tightened her grip on Pansy's hand and took him upstairs to his little girl's bedroom at the end of the corridor. She clipped on and locked the little pink chastity cage on his clitty, tucked him into bed and kissed him full on the lips. She slid her hand down under the covers to his sissy balls. She massaged her fingertips into them. Pansy reached up and put his arms around her neck. She untangled them and laid them out by his side. She stared at him for a few moments. Her naked breasts hung close to his chin.

"Pansy Princess. How many times do I have to tell you not to touch Goddess with your naughty femboy hands." She slapped his face. A smile built on her lips. "Naughty little girl, maybe Mr Benedict will have to discipline you."

Pansy looked away. "No."

"No what, Princess?" Her voice was silky and gentle. "Goddess?"

"No, Goddess."

"Good girl." She dragged the pink cartoon princess bed covers back to expose his panties and the tiny bulge at the front. She moved her hand down, pulled the front of his panties down and tucked them under his little balls. "Let's see how little *Miss Clitty* is doing, shall we?"

She moved in close to inspect his cage and balls. She prodded at his little balls and Pansy groaned a slow deep moan, his penis hard against the cage bars. "I think *Miss Clitty* want to cum but there's no room for her to get erect."

Pansy pushed himself up. He nodded. He saw her thick rich blonde hair hanging over his genitals, her lips an inch away from the end of his cage. Her cool minty breath tingled the exposed end. She blew against it softly, looked back at him and smiled.

"Yes, Goddess, I want to cum. It's aching. Please take off my cage and help me to cum."

Gemma stroked the end slit with one finger through the end of the cage. "I thought she wanted to cum, Pansy," she said. She ran her finger up and down his balls then circled it back on the slit at the end hole of the cage. Pansy closed his eyes at the sensations from her soft fingertips. She moved in close, her mouth open. "Would you like Goddess to take the cage off and suck on *Miss Clitty*? Like I used to before you became a proper sissy femboy."

He nodded vigorously and willed it to happen. She moved her mouth over the end of the cage and she felt her warm moist breath over his caged clitty. Her tongue was almost at his slit and her fingers hovered around the cage lock. She pushed the cage key into the lock. Any moment now, the cage would fall off and her lips would go around his erection and the ecstasy would begin. Her hair tickled against his soft balls, her breath blasted again on his sensitive clitty head. His dry throat *clucked*. He felt his ejaculation about to burst. As soon as she had her lips there and her tongue on the end. Soon his cage would fall away and her mouth would close around his erection and he'd explode into her mouth.

Why didn't she finish it? Why didn't she unlock him and put her mouth on it? He felt her breathing on his penis head through the cage and the key around the lock. Now. She moved her head back and forth, her blonde hair dragged over his crotch and balls, teasing, tickling. She was giving a blow job to his cage but he could feel nothing on his clitty skin. She twisted the key to unlock the cage and then twisted it back to lock it.

She moved her head from side to side, her hair swayed over his little erection through the cage bars and across his delicate sensitive sissy balls. It would take one touch from her tongue and her lips and it would be over. A single flick of her tongue, the feel of her teeth. His ejaculation was on the brink. Any moment now.

She sat up. His clitty twitched, trapped inside the pink bars. One more blast from her breath, one tiny flick of her tongue. That was all he needed. But she'd stopped and was watching him with a wry grin. He gasped in desperation, this was agony. Rain hit the window outside with a gush. A crack of thunder sounded in the distance. He was on the point of sexual explosion but with nothing to press the button.

"Time for Pansy's beauty sleep," Gemma said.

"He sat up. "But? What? No?"

Gemma rubbed his cheek and touched his lips. "Yes, I know, Princess Petal, we can't have you cumming. That's not very feminine, is it?" She made an exaggerated fake shudder and smiled. "Nasty sissy juices. *Urgh*." She giggled as if making a shared joke.

She laid a hand on the cock cage. "I locked little *Miss Clitty* away for good loving reasons." She tapped the small cage. "In case you have any naughty urges to touch *Miss Clitty* in the night when I'm not here to look after your best interests. And your best interests are that you don't make a sissy mess." Gemma tucked him tightly in bed and kissed him on the forehead. She got up and walked to the door and her hand hovered over the light switch. She stood, one leg bent, her voluminous breasts large and firm. Her triangle of pubic hair was neatly trimmed and blond. He remembered when he had access to that honey pot. No more. She tilted her head to one side and her steel-blue eyes glinted in the light, a wide smile, a line of perfect teeth. "Goodnight, darling Pansy Princess. Sleep tight and don't let the bedbugs bite."

Pansy mumbled under his breath. She switched the light switch off. Someone else entered the room. A flash of lightning lit the room through the thin curtains for half a second. It illuminated Dr Fiona who sat on the bed. Another flash illuminated the poster of a naked young man with a large erect shaved cock on the wall above his bed. The thunder rolled, it was closer this time. Dr Fiona took his hand. Another flash of lightning and he saw her kind smile. She took his hand in both hers.

Gemma's bare feet padded down the hallway to the master bedroom. Benedict's deep voice murmured indistinctly. Several slurps sounded. A few seconds later, he heard bedsprings bounce and high-pitched giggles echo down the hall. The squeal of the bedsprings became more regular, slow and rhythmic. Gemma's shrill voice called out, "*Oh oh oh, you sex lover. What a fantastic cock you have. It's filling me up.*" Her squeals rang down the hall and swirled around his bedroom. A deep-voiced groan followed and the bedspring squeals sped up, faster, more energetic.

Dr Fiona's hand squeezed his as the sounds of passionate sex echoed down the corridor. Lightning flashed twice and thunder banged directly overhead, shaking Pansy's room. "It sounds like Mr Benedict and your wife have consummated their relationship, Pansy." Dr Fiona rubbed her hand against his.

Voices whispered and floated to his ears. He heard Gemma say, "*I love you, Robert. You're so much more masculine than my pathetic femboy husband.*" Had he heard that right? Had Gemma just said, *I love you* to Benedict? It must have been a mistake, he wasn't with her. His ears must be playing tricks in the darkness and the storm.

"Yes." Benedict's bass voice rumbled loud and clear. Lightning and thunder rattled the windows. "I love you too, Gemma."

Chapter 12: Sissy School

PANSY STARTED AT DR Fiona's Sissy Institute the next morning. Jerome picked Pansy up at 7.45am and drove him to Dr Fiona's sissy school. Jerome held Pansy's hand as Gemma had instructed him and delivered him to Dr Fiona Boleyn-Hunter in the classroom.

Pansy was dressed in the school uniform of a pleated school miniskirt in red tartan plaid, a fitted white blouse and white socks to below his knee with a pink frill around the top. His shoes were black and had a thick one-inch heel with a single strap and a large buckle on the front. His long brown hair was brushed to his shoulders. The other three students in the classroom were dressed in identical uniforms.

Jerome left him and he stood at the front with his hands over his skirt and his head down. A low watery sun filtered through the wide classroom windows. A tall elegant woman was getting into a long silver car a few feet from the window. He guessed she was a wife who had just dropped her sissy husband off at school for the day. A sixth sense made her look up and they fixed eyes for a long moment. The lady looked down at his skirt and then up. Her mouth twisted in a smirk and she got in and closed the car door.

He felt uncomfortable in front of his fellow sissy students, more so with the two female tutors who were standing at the side of the room with arms crossed.

The school principal, Dr Fiona Boleyn-Hunter BA, MA, PhD, stood next to him. She held a short cane with a curved handle and tapped it in the palm of one hand. "I'd like you to welcome Pansy Gold to the school," she said, looking down at him through black rectangular glasses and using his wife's original name.

Pansy struggled to keep his eyes off Dr Fiona's never-ending legs. Despite being the school principal, she wore a minuscule black pencil skirt that seemed to have been sprayed on. She wore black stockings and high heels with stilettos made of shining chrome metal.

"Pansy has been sent here by her charming wife to learn how to become a well-behaved submissive little sissy and to learn how to become more girly. Dr Fiona tapped the cane in her hand as she spoke. "Pansy has a tiny clitty and girly balls which is why she was useless to his wife as anything other than a financial source and a sissy housemaid."

Pansy choked and looked up. A stifled snigger sounded from one of the other students. He saw her put a large wide hand with pink painted nails over her mouth. Her long straightened fair hair hung down to her shoulders. One of the tutors raised a finger at the student and the student swallowed hard, a large Adam's apple moving up then down again.

Dr Fiona raised the front of Pansy's skirt with her cane and held it up. All eyes zeroed in on the front of Pansy's navy blue school panties. A slight bump in an otherwise flat crotch area.

"Pull down your panties, Pansy," Dr Fiona said.

Pansy's eyes widened in shock. "Excuse me, Madam?"

Her cane swished through the air and caught him across one smooth bare thigh. Pansy squealed from the stinging shock. A red weal raised

"You heard me, sissy." Dr Fiona's voice was deep and firm. "At my institute, you must follow every instruction I give without delay." She put her cane to the front of his skirt and raised it once more. The three sissies there struggled to keep straight faces. The other students were the blond one, a small pretty sissy with an angular face and a tall gangly sissy. The two tutors were of equal height, one was slim and boyish-looking with short blond hair. The other was dark skinned and curvy with large breasts and long wavy brown hair.

Dr Fiona cleared her throat. Pansy tucked his thumbs into the waistband of his panties, breathed in and pulled them down. They fell to his ankles.

There was another stifled snigger and an *"oh"* from the boyish tutor. Pansy looked down with shame. His little penis hung loose and soft in front of two golf-ball-like testicles.

"This was Pansy's wife's problem and part of the reason she's here." Dr Fiona stared at Pansy's genitals, a sneer on her lips. "Would anyone care to guess how long her little clitty is?"

The tall sissy shot a hand up.

"Yes, Sindy," Dr Fiona said.

"Two inches?"

"Very good." Dr Fiona leaned over and nodded.

Pansy shuddered at what was happening. It was bad enough to be standing in a little girl's school uniform; having her penis exhibited and discussed was a whole new level.

"And how long would you guess it to be when hard?"

The last thing Pansy could imagine was being erect and excited at this moment in this situation.

Dr Fiona pointed at Sindy, the sniggering sissy with her free hand. Her cane maintained Pansy's skirt up. "Sindy, come here."

Sindy stared at her a moment and stood up slowly, his chair scraping on the floor. He shuffled to Dr Fiona and stood with his head down. Pansy would never have guessed that Sindy was a sissy, in other circumstances he would have given him a second look. And a third. Sindy's legs were long, slim and feminine. He had real breasts; Pansy could see the mounds from his unbuttoned blouse. His face was small and pretty with well-applied makeup.

"You seem to think this is so funny, you can rub her clitty to see how it looks when hard."

His head shot up to her. "Pardon?"

Her can swished over his thighs and he jumped with a squeal like a little piglet. She returned her cane to lift Pansy's skirt front.

This can't be happening, thought Pansy. It was. Sindy knelt and Pansy jumped as he put two cold fingers on his small penis.

"Rub it, sissy, so we can all see how big it is when it's hard." Dr Fiona's voice was curt.

A public masturbation? This was awful. Pansy hadn't cum for some time and Gemma, his wife, had teased him mercilessly, bringing him to the point then stopping. At night, she locked him in a cock cage. He tried to think of the positive, this was a chance for release and how he needed that right now.

Pansy closed his eyes and tried to think about his wife, the former supermodel. Tall blond, sexy and beautiful. He imagined they were her fingers on his penis. It grew. He heard another snigger and a long *'ohhhh'* from a female voice. Sindy seemed to know what he was doing as waves of pleasure now fell through Pansy. His eyes screwed tight, the vision of Gemma's long slender fingers on his foreskin ran through his mind: rubbing, pulling, gentle and sensuous.

He felt a warmth in his balls, a twang in his stomach. His juices were reaching boiling point, he was on the cusp, the edge of an explosion. Days of build-up were about to shatter and erupt. Any instant.

Sindy's hands fell away. Pansy flung his eyes open. "What?"

His little erection stood out straight and firm.

"About four inches," one of the tutors said.

Dr Fiona nodded. "More like three, I'd say. Tiny, tiny, tiny."

"What?" Pansy said again.

Fiona took the cane away from his skirt hem and poked it on his chest. "Your lovely wife has stipulated that you are not to cum." Dr Fiona's voice rumbled.

"What?" Pansy couldn't comprehend, he was bursting, desperate. A whiff of breeze would be all it took.

"Pull your panties up and take your seat, Pansy, time for lessons." Dr Fiona walked to the classroom door."

"But, Madam, I'm desperate."

Dr Fiona ignored him and walked to the door to leave the room. She stopped and turned back. "Anne."

The tall blond tutor stepped forward. "Yes, Principal."

"Have one of the sissy students rub Pansy every morning first thing and every afternoon at the end of class. Bring her to the brink and stop. It's an important element of her psychological rebuilding. Keeps her on edge and compliant and she'll become accustomed to never cumming."

"Yes of course, Principal."

Dr Fiona left the room.

Pansy sat, his penis still hard and tingling. He had a small damp patch on the front of his panties. He slumped in his seat. Anne began by explaining that the first lesson was on how to speak like a little girl. Her words faded into the background. Ejaculation was the only thought on Pansy's mind. And that was not going to happen any time soon.

Chapter 13: Sissy Lessons

Now Pansy was attending Dr Fiona's Sissy Institute, he couldn't go to the office. Gemma appointed his deputy to take over the running of the company for the unforeseeable future. At Sissy School, Pansy learnt how to behave like a proper little girl. He was given constant and repetitive practice by the tutors. They taught him how to sit, how to wait for a lady to speak first, how to curtsey and how to sit down on the toilet and pee like a girl.

Pansy had daily elocution lessons on how to speak like a little girl. The teachers taught him how to speak in a higher tone and with a more feminine lilt. Dr Fiona put Pansy on a special diet at the school. Breakfast at school was at 8.30 am and consisted of four slices of refined white bread. This was covered with sweet dripping syrup. Coffee was made with full-fat milk and with two spoonfuls of white refined sugar. Lunch was a full-sized pizza or a burger served with fried potatoes. Dessert was ice cream and chocolate cake. The afternoon snacks were full-sugar cola and sweet biscuits.

Pansy's bottom and hip size shot up six inches in six months. His bottom filled out and became large and rounded. His flat chest drooped into small fatty sacks like an old woman's tits. Gemma liked to call him Chubby Pansy Princess or her cute chubby sissy. Gemma made him leave the house in the girly uniform and get into the car on the drive where Jerome would wait in the driver seat.

The classes always had two or three female tutors and three other sissy students. Pansy had to drop his panties every morning after breakfast at the front of the class and lift his skirt. The tutors would laugh at his clitty and girly balls and encourage the other students to tell them how small and girly Pansy's genitals were. Every day the tutors chose a sissy student to rub Pansy's clitty with their fingers. The tutors observed closely to see when he was about to cum when they made them stop. Pansy found he was becoming used to not cumming and the masturbation sessions became long and longer.

Pansy's classes finished at 5pm. Before leaving, the tutors made Pansy repeat the curtailed morning masturbation session. Sometimes Dr Fiona joined the session to observe.

Once Jerome had taken him home, Gemma gave Pansy one of several outfits to change into: cheerleader, ballet dancer, a fairy with wings or French maid. Dr Fiona also introduced new outfits: an air hostess, a bunny girl with large rabbit ears on Pansy's head and various little girls' party dresses and princess outfits. Sometimes if she was in the mood, she'd drop her panties and lift her skirt and tell Jerome to make love to her.

Gemma assumed ownership although left the day-to-day running to his deputy. of Pansy's company to Benedict now Pansy attended Dr Fiona's sissy institute. Robert Benedict moved into their house and slept in the main bedroom with Gemma. Benedict often arrived home stressed after a heavy day running his company and Gemma told Pansy it was his job to help to de-stress him once he got in. Pansy would have to rush to the door and take Benedict's coat. Pansy had to make him a drink and bring the newspaper or a book while Benedict relaxed in the evenings and to serve them both for dinner.

One day, after six months of this new lifestyle, Pansy heard Benedict's car pull up into the driveway. It was earlier than usual as it was just after 7pm. Pansy rushed to the hall to receive him and wait for his instructions: whisky or tea, newspaper or book in the living room.

That night, Gemma had dressed Pansy in a little girl's party dress. The dress was pink with ***Little Princess*** printed on the front. He wore white ankle-high socks and pink flat ballet shoes. His make-up was heavier than usual and the lipstick was thick and red. Pansy's ears had been pierced at Sissy School and he now wore wide hoop earrings. His hair was much longer and ran down his back.

Benedict breezed in through the front door, a broad smile on his face. He saw Pansy waiting and wiped both sides of his moustache. Pansy was relieved that Benedict was not so stressed this evening, maybe he wouldn't have to run around so much for his wife's lover. Gemma joined them in the hall, which wasn't unusual. Her eyes sparkled as she looked up at her lover. Pansy's stomach twisted at seeing her passion for Robert Benedict.

Something was different and Pansy spotted it. Benedict and Gemma looked pleased with themselves. Instead of demanding a whisky, Robert put his arms around Gemma. They gazed into each other's eyes. Even after six months, it hurt to see them this way and Pansy's chest pained with desire for her. His former rival and his hot sexy wife had taken over his home. They looked down at Pansy and their smiles grew wider. What was going on?

"We've got something wonderful to tell you, Pansy puff," said Gemma with a glint in her eye.

They looked at each other again, Benedict wiped his moustache again in that way that annoyed Pansy so much.

"I'm pregnant," Gemma said.

Pansy's mouth dropped open. He stopped breathing, a pain jolted across his chest. He caught his breath and thought he might faint.

"Robert and I are going to have a baby. Isn't that wonderful, Pansy? You were so incompetent as a lover, you must be happy for me to have found such great sex with Robert."

Pansy froze and his skin crawled cold. A baby? That wasn't wonderful. It was one thing to play out this cuckold game of Gemma's hoping that, one day, she would get bored of it and come back to him as she had with Karlene and Daniel. But having a baby with her lover was another thing entirely, something more permanent. His mind raced. This was permanent. A baby.

Gemma interrupted his thoughts. "I have even more great news, Pansy. I've spoken to Dr Fiona and they are going to teach you how to care for our baby. Isn't that wonderful? You'll be our live-in nanny as well as the house girl of course."

This wasn't wonderful.

"And what's more, since I'll be involved in having a baby, I'm turning over the running of the company to Robert." She leaned down and tweaked his soft little balls through his panties. "You're going to be far too busy caring for our beautiful new baby to worry about running a company, my flabby little cuckold femboy." A smile spread across her beautiful lips.

Pansy ran a hand through his long hair. A baby? His wife and smarmy Benedict? He didn't know what to think. Pansy couldn't breathe.

Benedict and Gemma stared into each other's eyes.

Chapter 14: The Nightmare

He woke with sweat soaking his face. His heart thumped against his chest like a native war drum. He sat up. He was in the king-sized bed in the master bedroom. That was odd, what was he doing here? He turned to his right and saw Gemma lying next to him fast asleep, her breathing deep and steady. His head thumped. What was going on? He couldn't remember. Had he had a bad dream? Where was Robert Benedict? He reached down to his penis and balls. They were not locked away. They felt smaller. It must be colder than he realised.

He looked down at his nightwear. He was dressed in a short pink nightie with **PRETTY PRINCESS** printed on the front in bright red. He felt his hair. It was long and thick and down his back. He put his fingernails up to his eyes. They were long and coloured bright pink. He ripped the covers back. His bottom and stomach were large and plump. He touched his chest. It was hairless but he had two obvious lumps like a young girl's breasts. They were small tits, there was no doubt. He was sleepy, maybe he was still dreaming.

"What are you doing, sweetie? It's Saturday." Gemma's voice was dreamy and soft; her arm flowed over him and she snuggled her head into him tight. Her hand went to his dick and she stroked it softly. He felt her fingers on his smooth skin. He had no pubic hair. In fact, it all felt too smooth, as if he'd had electrolysis or something. He waited for her to clamp his balls hard or slap them. Instead, she rubbed them with gentle affectionate swirls. Her hand moved back to his penis and she rubbed it and it sprang hard. His head hurt with confusion.

"*Oooh*," she cooed. "Something's hard and ready. I'm surprised it still works, especially as it's even smaller than before now."

He didn't understand. What did that mean? "What am I doing here? I was, I was...." He trailed off. He was dressed as Pansy with a smooth body and long hair but he was in bed with Gemma. He hadn't been in the same bed as Gemma for months.

"Oh Sweetie, you seem stressed, were having a bad dream? Never mind, relax, lay back. I'll take care of that nasty dream for you." She sat up and sat astride him and onto his hard little penis.

He rubbed his eyes then his head: it hurt like a migraine or a hangover. His mouth was dry. As he rubbed his eyes, Gemma moved up and down on him; she swirled a hand through her hair and her head lolled back and sideways. Her face was distant and dreamy. She closed her eyes. He felt her vagina around his dick. It was warm and juicy; he hadn't felt that for a long time. He laid back. It was not the time to try to understand but to enjoy this moment with his wife. This had to be a dream though. He'd wake up any moment.

She rubbed and ground herself into him. Waves of pleasure engulfed him, his headache fell away. Surges of electricity built in his stomach and balls, rising up and into his erection.

He waited for her to stop as he reached the brink. His juices reached the cusp, he was about to explode. Surely she was going to stop, to hold him at that point. She continued to grind and manoeuvre her bottom around his crotch. He didn't cum. It was as if he had been conditioned not to cum. He had.

"Mummy? Mummy?" A little girl's voice called in the distance.

Gemma rolled off and cuddled deeply into him. His erection throbbed on the brink. "Aren't you going to see to her, dear? Isn't that your job? I'll finish myself off with a dildo."

What the hell was going on? Who was that little girl?

"Mummy?" The little girl's voice was louder this time, more desperate. It seemed to be coming from the other side of their bedroom door.

He pulled back from his wife. "Who on Earth is that?"

Gemma stared at him. "What's the matter with you today, Pansy? Get up and see to her"

"Pansy?" he asked, his mind was mixed up, he was getting contradicting messages. Nothing made any sense. He was in bed with his wife and yet she called him Pansy and he was still dressed as a sissy. And he had tits.

Gemma rubbed his face and kissed him gently on the lips. "What else would I call you, darling?" She looked concerned. Are you OK, would you like me to get you something? A glass of water, Ibuprofen? You had far too much wine last night. I had to put you to bed."

"*Mummy,*" the young girl's voice screeched out, desperate. A hand banged on the bedroom door.

He sat up, hands flat on the mattress. "Who the hell is that little girl, Gemma?"

She sat up next to him, her smile fell away. "What is the matter with you this morning, Pansy? Who the hell do you think she is?"

"I have no idea." He rubbed his forehead hard with the palm of his hand, coloured migraine flashes shot through the back of his eyes and his temples throbbed. His mind was cloudy but some memories were flitting back.

"The doctor said you might get these moments of confusion with the pills to start with."

"What tablets," he asked with a screech.

"Mummy." Two

Gemma's face flashed with anger. She pushed herself up on her elbows. Her eyes flashed anger. "Get up now, Pansy, or do you want me to spank you and then squeeze your sissy little balls?"

"What? What?" he asked digging the heels of his hands in both eyes.

"Go and see what little Roberta wants."

· · ✿ · ·

THE END

This is the final book of the series, Sissy Husband. I hope you enjoyed the story of Pansy. Please leave me a review on the site you bought this novella from.

• • ◦‍⁂‍◦ • •

Subscribe to my blog charting my real-life FLR and forced feminisation lifestyle with my feminised husband Alice here: www.ladyalexauk.com[1]
You can also subscribe to my newsletter from my blog by clicking on the side bar and entering your email:
<u>*www.ladyalexauk.com*</u>
Thank you
Lady Alexa

Don't miss out!

Visit the website below and you can sign up to receive emails whenever Lady Alexa publishes a new book. There's no charge and no obligation.

https://books2read.com/r/B-A-JTBM-OTWJF

BOOKS 2 READ

Connecting independent readers to independent writers.

2. https://books2read.com/u/bokkk0

3. https://books2read.com/u/bokkk0

original was a forced feminisation and sissification story where a husband is feminised by a Mistress and his wife as a double act. They turn him into a submissive and cuckolded sissy.

This novel contains explicit scenes of a sexual nature including forced male to female gender transformation, female domination, humiliation, CFNM, BDSM, spanking and reluctant feminisation. All characters in this story are aged 18 and over.

Strictly for adults aged 18 and over or the age of maturity in your country.

Read more at https://www.ladyalexauk.com.

Also by Lady Alexa

A Sissy Cuckold Husband
Sissy Husband 3

Becoming Joanne
Becoming Joanne 1
Becoming Joanne 2
Becoming Joanne 3

Femboy Love
Femboy Love 1

Feminized and Pretty
Feminized and Pretty 1
Feminized and Pretty 3
Feminized and Pretty 4

Forced Feminization

Forced Feminization Bundle 1

Lockdown Feminization
Lockdown Feminization 3
Lockdown Feminization 1

Sissy femboy transgender husband
SIssy Husband 1
Sissy Husband 4

Sissy Princess
Sissy Princess 2
Sissy Princess 1

Stepmother's Sissy
Stepmother's Sissy
Stepmother's Sissy 2
Stepmother's Sissy 3

Standalone
A Very Dominant Woman
Sissy Pink

About the Author

I am an author and blogger on female led relationships, encouraged feminization and femdom and other erotica.

Read more at https://www.ladyalexauk.com.